Discover the unusual, but always intriguing, world of Lynn Michaels and her characters

The reviewers at *Rendezvous* said about her first Temptation title, *Remembrance:* “Come along... on a trip filled with love and laughter and at times chills and thrills. I adored the characters, even the rotten ones, and had a darn good time sharing their lives.”

Lynn's next book, *Second Sight,* also received raves. *Romantic Times* said: “Lynn Michaels skillfully adds a mystical touch as she sensitively explores the boy hidden inside the man in this genuine tug-at-your-heartstrings love story. 4+” *Rendezvous* concurred. “This is a jim-dandy story with a tongue-in-cheek flavor to it, and you can't help but like the whole darn bunch of characters. Ms. Michaels has created another tale to be reread often. Loved it.”

And of the action-packed *The Patriot, Rendezvous* declared: “It's been a long time since I've been this enthusiastic about a romance.... This book has adventure, mystery, and romance.... Fantastic!” *Romantic Times* agreed: “Lynn Michaels brings us action-packed adventure.... Wonderful energy between these tough, but tender lovers. A marvelous read!”

Talented and versatile **Lynn Michaels** loves a challenge, and when we discussed the Passion's Quest project with her, she jumped at the chance to choose Earth as her element. While she joked about giant earthworms roaming the planet, challenging Godzilla for supremacy, we were thrilled with the nonstop action and the daring, opinionated and very passionate hero and heroine she created.

Lynn, her husband and their two boys make their home in Missouri. She would love to hear from her readers.

Lynn Michaels
c/o Harlequin Temptation
225 Duncan Mill Road
Don Mills, Ontario, Canada
M3B 3K9

Books by Lynn Michaels

HARLEQUIN TEMPTATION

304–REMEMBRANCE
405–THE PATRIOT
449–SECOND SIGHT

AFTERSHOCK

LYNN MICHAELS

Harlequin Books

TORONTO • NEW YORK • LONDON
AMSTERDAM • PARIS • SYDNEY • HAMBURG
STOCKHOLM • ATHENS • TOKYO • MILAN
MADRID • WARSAW • BUDAPEST • AUCKLAND

For both Bettys, Christine, Chelle, Connie, Nora and Rosie.
Thanks guys. You're the best.

ISBN 0-373-25581-0

AFTERSHOCK

This edition published by arrangement with Harlequin Enterprises B. V.

Printed in U.S.A.

Prologue

HE DIDN'T HAVE much time. They'd be here any minute. Yesterday, after he'd hung up on Smith, the man he'd never seen but whose money he'd been taking for the last five years, he'd realized that this time they'd come for sure.

The first thing he did was let his staff go, writing them fat checks with Smith's money, spinning them a yarn about closing the lab while he field-tested the TAQ box. Of course they believed him. Dr. Addison Wexler, Nobel laureate, didn't lie. The last one had left, headed for Barstow, California, the nearest point of civilization, less than three hours ago.

He'd then activated the lab security net, a highly sensitive and sophisticated system that would alert him to ground or air approach within a seven-mile radius of the compound. It had yet to sound the alarm; still, he felt sweat on his forehead. The virus disk was ready. It would take him less than two minutes, about all the time he figured he'd have once the sirens blew, to feed it to the mainframe and reduce its memory to simple-minded gibberish.

He'd already destroyed all the backup files. He'd sent Smith fakes as periodic progress reports. They contained enough dead-end equations to flummox whoever Smith brought in to try to duplicate his work. No scientist ever revealed all his research to anyone. Not even to his own mother. Sheridan had, and look where it had gotten him. Sheridan had been a fool, but so had he—an arrogant, greedy fool.

Wexler sat waiting in the middle of the main lab. There were only three last things to do. Through the heavily tinted, foot-thick glass surrounding him, the Mojave Desert stretched to the horizon in all directions. Anne had loved the desert, and so he'd built his lab here. He was glad she was dead, glad Rockie was in Spain filming a movie. Neither one of them would have left him to face this alone.

There were steel shields he could drop, installed at Smith's insistence. There were vault doors he could shut and lock, but he didn't see the point. Let them come. Let it end.

He picked up a ball peen hammer from the stainless-steel lab table. Beside it lay a nine millimeter semiautomatic, loaded with a single bullet, and the two prototypes of the TAQ box, the Tremor and Quake warning device. Five years' research, the best work he—and Sheridan—had ever done. In Smith's hands—Armageddon.

The phone rang as Wexler lifted the hammer. He stared, startled, at the light blinking on his private line. Only two people had the number. One he wished to God he'd never heard of, the other he'd give his last five years to see one more time. He put the hammer down, picked up the phone and said hello.

"*Buenos días*, Dad," his daughter said. "I'm home."

"Rockie." He closed his eyes and saw her dark pixie hair spiked around her face and Anne's green eyes. "Back a little early, aren't you?"

"I wouldn't take my clothes off, so I got fired."

"In an aliens from Jupiter movie they wanted nudity?"

"Not in the movie. In the director's trailer." He heard her pause and puff on a cigarette. "So I thought I'd come home. Maybe tinker in the lab, see if I couldn't blow it up like I just blew up my acting career. I mean for good, Dad, if you still want me."

There were tears in her voice. In Wexler's throat, too, but he gulped them back and wiped a hand over his mustache and mouth. Before he'd gotten involved with Smith and the TAQ box, he'd dreamed of having Rockie take Anne's place.

"C'mon, Rockie. Buck up," he said, his gaze falling on the gun. "Wexlers never quit."

"This one has. I want to come home, Dad. I stink as an actress. I want to put that degree in chemistry you said I'd be smart to have, just in case, to good use." She paused, puffing on her cigarette again. He wished she'd quit smoking. "Unless you don't want me, unless you're afraid I'll get bored and take off for New York and leave you high and dry."

"I've always wanted you here, Rockie. You know that. It's just that—"

The alarm sounded, spinning Wexler around on his lab stool. Three blips blinked across the security screen, coming hard and fast in a wedge from the northwest.

"Dad?" Rockie's voice sharpened. "Why is the alarm going off?"

"Dust storm, honey." Wexler stretched toward the console and punched a button to silence the sirens. "Nothing to worry about."

"Wrong time of year for dust storms, Dad. What's going on? What's the matter?"

"I don't have time to explain." The receiver tucked between his shoulder and jaw, Wexler wheeled his stool across the lab, snatched up the disk and fed it to the mainframe. "I left a message on your machine earlier and a phone number I want you to call the second we hang up. Do you understand? The *second* we hang up."

"You're scaring me, Dad. I'm coming out there. The Jeep is all packed. I'll be there in—"

"I won't be here, Rockie. I'm going away for a while."

Forever qualified as a while. Wexler's fingers flew across the keyboard. He could hear the eggbeater rhythm of the helicopters, could see the dust storm swirling for real outside the windows as they swooped to the ground inside the security fence.

"It's the TAQ box, isn't it? And that weird guy Smith. Dad, you *promised* me—"

"I love you, Rockie. Goodbye."

Though it took precious seconds, Wexler hung up the receiver, made sure the connection had broken, then lifted it again and left it off the hook. He picked up the hammer, dropped it, bent to retrieve it and froze in midreach when he heard the metallic click of an automatic weapon being cocked.

Wexler glanced up at the lab doorway. The biggest man he'd ever seen stood there with an Uzi pointed at him. The barbarian had close-cut brown hair and wore desert fatigues. His hands were so large the Uzi looked like a toy.

Wexler wet his dry lips. "Are you Smith?"

"No, Dr. Wexler." He smiled, his voice pleasant. "My friends call me Conan."

1

NOTHING KEPT Nevin Maxwell from his desk. Not even a killer hangover. Delayed him, yes. It was eleven-thirty when he left for his office. Normally, he was there by ten.

His head pounded throughout the drive into Manhattan. Every seam in the Long Island Expressway jarred him like a fist, made him swear to God he'd never do Elaine's until closing on a Tuesday night ever again. No matter how lush the redhead or how leggy the blonde.

He collected the mail from the lock box adjacent to the parking garage and rode the elevator up to the fourth floor. He didn't look at the letters—he never did until he was seated at his desk—just leaned against the back wall of the elevator car and rubbed his rocky stomach. The abdominal stretches he did twice a day had nearly torn him in half this morning. Ah, well. The blonde especially had been worth it.

The reception area of his two-room suite contained a desk no one ever used. The file cabinets lining the walls of his private office were there for appearance only. He started a pot of coffee, popped four aspirin-free painkillers and opened the drapes to let in the smog-dulled sunshine. When the coffee finished, he poured himself a mug and sat down at his desk to open the mail.

When line three, the hot line, rang, he picked it up with a curt "Maxwell."

"Kevin Maxwell? Of Maxwell and Associates, Private Investigations?"

A cautious young lady, despite the quaver in her voice.

"Nevin Maxwell," he replied, "of Maxwell and Associates, Private Consultations."

"This is Rockie Wexler. Do you know my father?"

His photographic memory never forgot a face or a name, though God knew there were dozens he'd love to. Wexler's was but one he wished he'd never heard.

"Yes, I know Dr. Addison Wexler."

"He told me to call you. I don't suppose you know why?"

"Where are you, Miss Wexler?"

"Los Angeles."

"And your father?"

"I'd hoped you could tell me."

Maxwell's temples began to pound again. It was too damn early in the day after too damn long a night for this.

"I haven't seen or spoken to your father in eight years, Miss Wexler. Good day."

He hung up. It took her forty-five seconds to call back. He let it ring seven times before he answered.

"Listen, you prick." Her voice no longer quavered with uncertainty, it shook with anger. "I called my father twenty minutes ago. In the middle of our conversation the alarms in the lab went off. He said he didn't have time to explain, that I should call the number he'd left on my answering machine. *Your number.* Then he hung up. I called back but he didn't answer, so I had the operator check. She said the line is out of order."

"Now we're getting somewhere, Miss Wexler."

"Damn straight. I did what he asked, I called you. Now I'm getting myself to Barstow as fast as I can."

"Miss Wexler—"

She slammed the phone down. The loud plastic crack made Maxwell wince. He broke the connection and punched a number in Springfield, Missouri. A machine answered: "You've reached Dr. Leslie Sheridan. My hours are eleven to noon and three to five Monday through Friday. Leave a message with your dorm name or phone number, or see me in my office. Earth Sciences building, second floor."

"This is Maxwell," he said after the beep and hung up.

Midway through pouring himself another cup of coffee, line two, the number given only to his operatives, rang. He answered on the third ring, "Good morning, Sherry."

"Whatever it is, Max, I can't. This is finals week."

"Teaching assistants are born to handle finals. Wexler's daughter just called me."

"Who caught up with him at last? Uncle Sam?"

"Doubtful." Maxwell repeated what Rockie had told him.

"Sounds like he finally screwed the wrong guy," Sheridan said when he finished, a hint of relish in his voice.

"Any idea who?" Maxwell asked.

"Pin Khadafi, Arafat and Saddam on a wall, close your eyes and throw a dart."

"What's he into? Oil?"

"Last I heard."

"You could be in Barstow by three."

One of the perks that came with working for Maxwell was access to a private fleet of Lear jets.

"And out of my ever-lovin' mind, Max."

"I assumed you'd want this one."

"You assumed wrong. Like I said, this is finals week."

Sheridan hung up. So did Maxwell and sipped his coffee. The pounding in his head was beginning to recede.

Sheridan couldn't, or wouldn't, be in Barstow by three. But he could make it by four.

2

ROCKIE WEXLER MADE it to Barstow by twelve-thirty. At a gas station she slapped down her plastic to fill the tank of her red Jeep Cherokee and the spare can she carried, buy five jugs of distilled water, two packs of cigarettes and gum to chew between smoke breaks.

She was self-indulgent, not stupid, and had sense enough not to smoke in the Jeep with twenty extra gallons of unleaded premium sloshing in the back. She was scared, too, but took time to top the fluid levels in the engine. Blowing a rod in the middle of the desert wouldn't help her save her father. If she got there in time.

Rockie squelched the thought. It took something very big moving very fast to activate the security net. Not a dust storm or the occasional jackrabbit that got hung up in the fence. The system was programmed to screen out that sort of thing. Too bad her father wasn't programmed to treat her like an adult.

She'd lived on her own for seven years now, had sense enough to know when something wasn't kosher, and smarts enough to pull the Jeep away from the pumps and check the tires—including the spare and the jack—and her gear. Sleeping bag and blankets, duffel bag full of clothes, first-aid and snakebite kits, food, rain gear, hiking boots, hat, infrared binoculars, two-man tent in desert camouflage, and shortwave radio.

Rockie hadn't spent twenty-six years as Addison Wexler's daughter and a decade as a Girl Scout for nothing. She believed in being prepared.

The last thing she checked was the steel bar from her dumbbells wedged beside her seat. A stuntman she knew who moonlighted as a self-defense instructor had taught her how to use it for more than arm curls.

Once she'd belted herself in behind the wheel, Rockie put on her sunglasses, folded a stick of sugarless peppermint into her mouth and turned out of Barstow and into the Mojave Desert. Her father's lab lay 152 miles away. As her mother used to say, out where Christ lost his overshoes.

Turning the CB to Channel 19 and the radar detector her father had reconditioned and given her for Christmas on wide sweep, Rockie pressed the accelerator to the floor. On its maximum setting, the scanner picked up anything that moved within a three-mile radius.

The oddball gift had made her wonder if her father might be in some kind of trouble. It wasn't the first time Rockie had wondered, or the first time that Addison Wexler had ended up in the soup. He had a history of it. A knack for it, some people said. Jealous types, Rockie used to think, but the .32 automatic tucked in the Jeep's glove compartment, a birthday gift from her father, and the two prototypes of the TAQ box he'd shown her a month before she'd left for Spain, had changed her mind.

"Just think," he'd said, his pale blue eyes glowing with excitement. "No more cities reduced to rubble, no more billions of dollars in damage and thousands of lives lost."

"Just think," she'd replied, tapping the red power knob on the control panel. "One little twist and you have billions of dollars in damage and thousands of lives lost."

"At its maximum setting, it would take the TAQ box decades to move a fault," he'd retorted defensively. "And it isn't calibrated for anything higher."

"Gimme a screwdriver and I'll fix that."

"You don't understand," he'd said stubbornly. "You're a chemist, not a geologist."

"I'm an actress, and I understand simple physics. I also know the government confiscated all quake-detection research of this type years ago. Labeled it dangerous and irresponsible. Probably locked it up with the flying saucers and little green men. How'd you get your hands on this?"

"Don't worry about the government," he'd said, ignoring her question. "The funding for this is very private."

So private it arrived in person with a chauffeur the size of a boxcar about twenty minutes later, in a limo with heavily tinted and probably bulletproof glass. Rockie had watched from the the second-story windows as a fair-haired man with a great tailor slid out of the back of the car and buttoned his pinstripe suit coat.

"Is that your benefactor, Mr. Smith?" she'd asked.

"No. His associate, Greer Hanlon," her father had replied with a frown. "I've never met Smith. Wait here, Rockie."

He'd gone outside to meet Hanlon. They didn't shake hands or smile. Until her father plucked a computer disk out of his lab-coat pocket. Then Hanlon smiled as he took it and gave Dr. Wexler a slim white envelope.

Throughout the exchange the chauffeur loomed silently, his big hands folded in front of him. He looked like Arnold Schwarzenegger's double. When he shut the limo door behind Hanlon, he glanced up at the lab windows. No way could he see her through the thick, tinted glass; still, Rockie drew back a step, certain that he had.

"Did you notice the bulge under the chauffeur's left arm?" she'd asked her father once the limo had gone and he'd peeked inside the envelope with a satisfied smile.

"What bulge?" He'd blinked at her, his eyes still dancing with zeros.

"The gun in the holster inside his jacket."

"Oh, that," he'd replied with a dismissive shrug.

"Don't you think it's odd that this mysterious Mr. Smith, who's so passionately committed to the welfare of humanity, employs hired thugs?"

"Rockie." He'd looked at her askance and shaken his head. "This isn't a Hollywood movie set. This is real life."

"That's what scares me."

It still did. Enough to make her wipe her sweaty hands one at a time on her jean-clad thighs as the low, half-moon ring of scrubby hills behind the lab compound came into view. When the Jeep's odometer told her she was within three miles of the security fence, Rockie flipped the radar detector from wide sweep to static scan. It was one of her father's more ingenious innovations, with a screen no bigger than a hand-held video game. It lit up like L.A. at night, with three flashing dots centered inside the area representing the lab compound.

Rockie opened the glove compartment, took the gun out, slipped it between her knees and wiped her hands on her thighs again. She wasn't sure she could scare anybody with it, except maybe herself, but she was sure as hell going to try.

A narrow, mile-long stretch of private blacktop road connected the lab to the two-lane state highway. The turnoff wasn't marked and was almost obscured by windblown sand and dirt. Rockie stopped, checked the drift for tire treads, saw none, and decided the blips on her screen must be helicopters.

Once she made the turn, she saw their rotors through her binoculars. The sun slid in long silver beams down their stationary blades, and flashed on the black steel muzzles of automatic rifles carried by half a dozen soldiers in desert fatigues walking the fence. Three more manned the gate.

Oh, hell. Now what?

Rockie dropped the binoculars in her lap and chewed her bottom lip. Her father was in trouble, all right, big trouble. The kind you ended up in if you crossed a guy who used an alias and employed a chauffeur who carried a gun.

If her mother were alive, this wouldn't be happening. Until her death five years ago, Rockie hadn't realized how deftly Anne Wexler had managed to keep her husband's ego-driven impulses in check. Since then, dear old Dad had run amok. The TAQ box and the prowling soldiers proved that.

This was her fault. Rockie knew it, just like she'd known, deep down, for a long time, that as an actress she made a good stand-in. She'd never be anything but second-rate, but Wexlers never quit. Or were too damn stupid to know when to quit. It was a rationalization—she knew that—and codependent as hell, but it gave Rockie enough courage to look through the binoculars again.

She could raise the local cops on the CB or the shortwave and tell them her father's phone was on the blink and there were helicopters in the yard. Big deal, they'd say. Wexler Technologies did a lot of work for the government. Soldiers and choppers at the lab weren't that unusual. Neither were nuts who'd been out in the desert sun too long. She'd need more information than she had to interest the cops, and the only way to get it was to present herself at the gates. But not as herself—as a nut who'd been out in the desert too long.

It was the same trick Rockie used to get herself through auditions, the bane of every actor's life. Pretending to be someone else was a breeze compared to being Rockie Wexler. She'd been trying to get a handle on who Rockie Wexler was for twenty-six years. If all she'd had to be was herself she might've managed it, but the world expected her to be Rockie Wexler, Dr. Addison Wexler's poised and brilliant daughter.

She had the brilliant part knocked, perfect SAT scores and an honors degree in chemistry to prove it. Neither one of which did her a whole lot of good at the moment. Tucking the gun beside her seat next to the binoculars, Rockie took a map out of the glove compartment and folded it open on the seat beside her.

"Look out, Meryl Streep, here I come," she said, putting a bewildered expression on her face, the Jeep in gear and her foot on the gas.

3

ROCKIE APPROACHED the gate slowly, as if she were lost, unsure where she was going, maybe looking for landmarks. She was looking, all right. Looking for any sign of her father, counting heads among the soldiers. There were three more besides the nine she'd already seen, lugging cardboard storage boxes out of the three-story lab building toward the helicopters.

They were Apaches, combat choppers. Complete with gun turrets and rocket launchers. Rockie wiped her hands on her jeans again, rolled down her window and flipped on the automatic door locks as she neared the gate. One of the soldiers stepped through to meet her.

A soldier with an M16 slung over his shoulder, a walkie-talkie, and with no name and no insignia on his fatigues. A mercenary, Rockie realized, watching him unclip the radio from his belt. She tried but couldn't lip-read the few curt words he spoke into it.

"Boy, am I glad to see you!" she gushed once he'd drawn close enough to the Jeep that she could count the sweat beads on his forehead. "This sure is a big desert! It seems even bigger when you're lost."

Rockie gave him a helpless I-can't-find-my-way-out-of-a-paper-bag smile and batted her lashes. The trooper stared back at her, unmoved, his expression as animated as a rock.

"Where are you headed?" he asked, craning his neck to look at the gear stacked in the back of the Jeep.

"Barstow, to meet my girlfriends," Rockie replied quickly. "We're going camping, but I forgot my compass and I got all turned around and—"

"Got a map?"

Rockie handed hers through the window. The trooper took it and bent his head over it. He had crew-cut blond hair and a Robert DeNiro mole on his left cheek.

"Are you a marine?"

The trooper glanced up at her. "No," he said, and looked back at the map.

"Too bad. My friend Peggy is nuts about marines. She was hoping we'd meet some. She says you guys go on maneuvers out here all the time and . . ."

Rockie rambled on about the mythical Peggy, one eye on the trooper, the other on the point guys slowly walking the fence and watching her. The rest of the dirty dozen were still loading the boxes that contained her father's research files into the choppers. Rockie knew what they were because she'd helped pack them up for storage.

If they had her father they wouldn't need the files, she reasoned, and felt her heart start to race. He'd told her he was going away for a while. He didn't say where, but Rockie suddenly knew and could have kicked herself. Her gaze lifted to the hills behind the compound, where her father had built an underground warehouse connected to the lab by a tunnel.

If she'd taken the time to think about it, she would've realized it was the only place he'd had the chance to run to. But Rockie hadn't thought about it, she'd reacted—

to the alarms and her own panic. *Brilliant but impulsive.* More than one of her college professors had said that about her, had written notes on her lab work such as, "In your rush to reach the solution you skipped vital steps."

She'd skipped a vital one here, all right—*thinking.* What a stupid idea this was. Only marginally dumber than believing she had what it took to make it big in the movies. Maybe she *had* been out in the sun too long.

Maybe the trooper had, too, or maybe he was stalling. A ten-year-old could've figured out the way to Barstow by now.

"Oh, there it is! I see it now!" She stuck her left arm out the window and pointed at the map. "That big red circle—that's Barstow."

The trooper's head snapped up at a wary, sideways angle. Rockie gave him a sheepish smile.

"Two heads are better than one, y'know. Thanks for your help, and have a nice day." She started to draw her left arm back inside the Jeep, but the trooper's hand clamped like a manacle around her wrist.

"This area is restricted," he said. "How'd you find it?"

"I just followed the road," she replied, fighting the urge to wrench free. "I figured it led someplace."

"Oh, yeah? Like where?"

"I dunno. A gas station, maybe, or—"

"In the middle of the Mojave Desert you expected to find a gas station?"

"Well, you're here, aren't you?"

So was Greer Hanlon's chauffeur. Rockie saw him over the trooper's left shoulder, smiling as he came unhurriedly through the gate.

"Good afternoon, Miss Wexler," he said pleasantly. "How nice of you to join us."

She wondered fleetingly if he *had* seen her through the lab window and decided no, no way. Not unless he had X-ray vision like Superman. She had a feeling he had no intention of letting her go. Not if he could help it.

"Tell this bozo to take his hand off me," she said.

Hanlon's chauffeur nodded to the trooper. When he let go of her wrist, she snatched her arm back inside the Jeep and clamped her hand around the wheel.

"Where's my father?" Rockie demanded, slipping her other hand in between the seats.

"In the lab waiting to see you," he replied.

Liar, Rockie thought. With the window down, the air conditioner had lost its battle with the hot desert air. Rockie was beginning to sweat, but Hanlon's muscle didn't have so much as a damp spot on his crisply creased fatigues. He had close-cut brown hair and brown eyes, and he kept smiling at her, even when he tried the door and found it locked.

"Please unlock the door, Miss Wexler," he said. "Then turn off the engine and put both hands on the wheel where I can see them."

"Unlock it yourself," Rockie retorted, her fingers brushing across the butt of the gun and the steel bar beside it. She hesitated, her gaze shifting toward the trooper's M16, then wrapped her fingers around the bar.

"As you wish," he replied, reaching inside the window.

Rockie waited until his hand and most of his thickly muscled forearm were completely inside the Jeep. Then she swung the bar with every ounce of strength she had—and missed. She felt the recoil of the blow that smashed and split the door padding in a jolt all the way up her arm. She couldn't believe she'd missed, that someone so big could move so fast, but she didn't hesitate. As Hanlon's chauffeur jumped nimbly away from the door, she drew back her arm and hurled the bar at his head.

She heard it whistle through the air and saw the trooper dive for the ground. She shoved the Jeep into gear and trod on the gas. There was enough wind drift on the road to spin the wheels and throw up a cloud of sand, enough to blind Hanlon's chauffeur as he made a leap at her door. In her side mirror, Rockie saw him spin away and throw an arm over his eyes.

She also saw the troopers at the gate raise their M16s. The muzzles flashed, and a row of sand exploded a foot or so in front of the Jeep. Trying not to think about the twenty gallons of unleaded premium strapped in the back, Rockie pushed the accelerator to the floor. The front tires bit sand, spun the wheel in her hands and threw up an even bigger cloud of grit. Another burst of fire from the M16s stitched a rip in the sand next to her door.

Rockie jerked the wheel to the right and felt the Jeep fishtail as the back end sluiced off the road. She'd been four-wheeling in the Mojave since she was fourteen and knew the little red Cherokee better than she knew herself. She let the Jeep slide and slither, the tires spinning and churning up enough dust for a sandstorm.

Choked by the cloud billowing through the window, and every bit as blind as she hoped the soldiers at the gate were by now, Rockie coughed and fumbled for the power button to shut the window. She found it, pressed it and heard the tinkle of glass breaking inside the door. Wonderful.

Batting dust out of her face, Rockie blinked into the rearview mirror and saw another burst of fire zip through the sand behind her, streaking like a heat-seeking missile toward the tail pipe of the Jeep. She cut the wheel hard to the right, bounced the Cherokee out of the sand, back onto the road, and smack in front of a white U.S. Postal Service mail truck.

If the postman hadn't stepped on the brake and Rockie on the gas, they would've collided head-on. They missed each other by inches, close enough that Rockie could see the mailman's eyes were blue. Yanking the wheel to the left, she skidded the Jeep around the truck and managed, just barely, to keep it from sliding sideways off the right-hand side of the road.

In her mirror, she saw Hanlon's chauffeur and the trooper come running and coughing out of the dust cloud dead in front of the mail truck. Which is what Rockie figured she'd be if not for the postman's timely arrival. She saw the trooper skid to a halt, her heart in her mouth until he lowered his rifle. Hanlon's chauffeur pinned a broad smile on his face and raised a friendly hand to the mailman.

The chauffeur's eyes, however, never left the fleeing red Jeep. They locked with Rockie's in the rearview mirror. Only for a second, just long enough to zip a shiver of dread up her spine, then she tore her gaze away and pushed hard on the gas pedal.

She doubted Hanlon's chauffeur would shoot a government employee and risk bringing every FBI agent in the state down on his neck. The postman was safe, but she wasn't. It wouldn't take long to make up a plausible story and send him on his way. Five, maybe ten minutes max, Rockie figured, before the Apaches were airborne and after her.

It was the long way around to the back entrance of the tunnel, but she stuck to the road. If the troopers had binoculars, they'd think she was running for Barstow, which is what Rockie wanted them to think.

A half mile down the road, a narrow, rutted trail that appeared to be little more than tire tracks left by a recent bunch of four-wheel-fanatics led back into the hills behind the lab. Rockie took the turn slowly and squarely to avoid telltale tire marks to show where the Jeep had left the blacktop.

Within a dozen yards the first steep slope of the hills began. Impulse screamed at her to floor it, but she didn't. Instead, she crawled the Jeep up the trail, checking in her mirror to make sure she wasn't leaving a here-I-am-come-and-get-me dust trail for the choppers to follow.

She counted seconds in her head—*four thousand twenty-one, four thousand twenty-two*—almost four and a half minutes, almost a hundred more yards of rocks and ruts between her and the top of the trail. *Four thousand twenty-six, four thousand twenty-seven—*

The track reared almost straight up in front of her, winding and twisting up the sharp flank of the hills. The Jeep bounced from rut to rock and back again. Sweat trickled down the back of Rockie's neck, made her clenched hands slippery on the wheel. *Five thousand one, five thousand two—*

She bit her tongue, swallowed her gum and tasted blood as the Jeep bounced through a last, nasty chuckhole and cleared the shoulder of the hills. Straining her ears for the *whup-whup-whup* of the Apaches taking flight, Rockie wheeled the Jeep off the track, cranking the wheel hard to the right to cut around and behind the hills.

The highway lay three hundred yards and a hundred or so feet below. There was very little sand up here, the dust storms saw to that. The ground was cement-hard earth and rock, impervious to tracks unless it was wet. Luckily, it hadn't rained in over a year.

Shoving the Jeep into Park, Rockie unlocked her seat belt and stretched toward the glove compartment. She opened it, grabbed her binoculars and what looked like a garage door opener with two control pads, kicked open her door, jumped to the ground and ran on shaky, threatening-to-buckle legs toward a small cleft between two boulders. *Five thousand thirty-eight, five thousand thirty-nine—*

Bracing herself on her elbows, Rockie raised the field glasses and peered over the edge. The lab lay about three-quarters of a mile below her. The Apaches still squatted in the yard, their doors open, the soldiers climbing aboard.

There was no sign of Hanlon's chauffeur or her father. He'd done it! He'd gotten away before they arrived. Relief swept through Rockie, but then the lab door opened and her father came out. Hanlon's chauffeur followed, pointing an Uzi at Wexler. Behind them came two troopers, carrying a coffin-domed black box between them, the case her father had built to transport the TAQ box prototypes to their field tests.

"Aw, shit, Dad," Rockie groaned, blinking away sudden hot tears that sprang in her eyes.

As he walked toward the closest Apache, her father's gaze lifted toward the hills. Behind him, Hanlon's chauffeur raised his head, looked Rockie square in the eye and smiled. There was no way he could see her, but still a jolt of panic shot through her. She wanted to scream, run back to the Jeep, grab her .32 and charge down the hill like John Wayne to rescue her father. The impulse was so strong it started her heart pounding in her ears, but Rockie checked it, holding the glasses steady until her father and the TAQ box prototypes were safely aboard the Apache.

This was real life, not a movie. Charging down the hill to save her father wouldn't save him. She'd only get herself captured—or worse. The best thing she could do was get herself out of sight, wait until Hanlon's chauffeur gave up looking for her, then holler for help on the CB.

Rockie turned around on her knees, head down, fumbling for the remote in the pocket of her denim shirt. Her fingers were shaking so badly she dropped it. She picked it up, swearing, moved her thumb over the left-hand switch and froze as her lowered gaze locked on a long, lean shadow spreading toward her on the rock-hard ground.

The shadow of a man, very tall and broad-shouldered. Wearing a baseball cap. With a gun in his hand.

4

"I SEE ADDISON HASN'T lost his love for gadgets," said the shadow. "It's nice to know some things never change."

Along with her gift for chemistry, Rockie had an ear for voices. Brief as her conversation with Nevin Maxwell had been, she recognized his chilly baritone. On the phone it had given her the willies. In person it gave her the creeps.

Cautiously, she raised just her eyes to look at him, blinking in the dazzling sunlight bouncing off his mirror-lens sunglasses and the muzzle of the gun in his right hand. His dark hair, where it stuck out around his ears beneath the royal blue Chicago Cubs baseball cap, gleamed with red highlights. His khaki shirt and faded jeans were streaked with dust and sweat.

Nothing with any sense moved on the Mojave at this time of day. Still as it was, Rockie had no trouble hearing the chopper rotors begin their slow spin and wind up for takeoff.

"Whatever that thing does, I suggest you use it," Maxwell said, nodding at the remote in her hand. "Unless you want to go with your father and Conan."

Hell, no, she didn't. But she wasn't sure she wanted to stay with this gun-toting stranger, either, despite the message her father had left on her answering machine: You can trust Maxwell. He's a coldhearted SOB, but he'll help you. He won't want to, because of me, but he will.

It wasn't much of a character reference—for her father or Nevin Maxwell, Rockie realized—but there wasn't time to ask to see his résumé. The warm-up whine of the Apaches had evened out into a throaty, ready-for-lift-off purr.

"Is Conan his real name?" she asked, pushing the left-hand switch on the remote as she scrambled to her feet.

"A nickname. Nobody knows his real name. Not even Interpol." Maxwell glanced toward the truck-size slab of wind-eroded and sand-pocked hillside slowly sliding open, then back at Rockie. "Very clever. Let's go."

Tucking his gun in a kidney holster, he turned and made quickly for the passenger side of the Jeep. Rockie started after him, then paused and took a last backward look at the lab. The Apaches were lifting slowly off the ground, dust devils swirling around their landing gear.

"Hang on, Dad. Wexlers never quit," she murmured, then hurried after Maxwell.

Sliding behind the wheel, Rockie flipped on the headlights and hot-footed the Jeep into the tunnel. She stepped on the brake as the back wheels rolled over an expansion joint and waited to make sure the door closed before pressing the right-hand switch that turned on the lights.

"I assume this connects to the lab." The overhead halide lamps slowly flickered to life and cast shadows across Maxwell's square jaw and straight nose. "What are the chances Conan found it?"

"Nil. Dad burned the blueprints," Rockie replied. "To access the tunnel from the lab you have to push the reset button on the microwave in the coffee room three times. The entrance is in the janitor's storage closet in the basement."

"Still paranoid after all these years," Maxwell said with a slow shake of his head.

"How do you know my father?" Rockie let off the brake.

The Jeep rolled forward about a foot before Maxwell said, "Hold it," and she stopped.

"Who else knows about this tunnel?"

"Nobody. Just me and Dad."

"Let's make sure. Wait here."

He pitched his sunglasses on the dash, turned his Cubs hat backward and drew his gun as he slid out of the Jeep and edged along the wall following the steep downward slope. A very cautious and evasive man, Rockie thought, wondering why he hadn't answered her question. The way her luck was running, Maxwell was another Mr. Smith out of her father's past.

There'd been two other Mr. Smiths she knew of for sure, a couple more she'd suspected. Private benefactors were like golden geese, her father said. So long as you fed them now and then they kept laying eggs. No government or corporate interference, no making do on inadequate budgets and worrying that your grant will be cut by a congressional committee or a dimwitted board of trustees. And most important to Addison Wexler, no one lurking in the wings to steal your glory.

While every scientist guarded his work, her father was—as Maxwell had said—paranoid. In the extreme. The lab security system was light-years ahead of anything the military had. The safeguards he used to protect his research were as intricate as a Gordian knot.

Just a harmless little kink, Rockie had thought. Sometimes exasperating, but as much a part of him as his blue eyes. Now she knew better. Now she knew he'd been taking precautions against a day like this, realized he'd been hedging his bets in case somebody like Conan came swooping down on him in choppers with gun turrets, rocket launchers and mercenaries. And she even knew why—the TAQ box.

A shiver crawled up the back of her neck, a combination of dread and the tunnel air beginning to circulate through the ventilation system. It came on automatically with the lights, recycling the air every three hours. Figuring she had enough trouble already without carbon monoxide poisoning, Rockie switched off the engine and the headlights.

"Smart girl." Maxwell appeared out of nowhere, opened the passenger door and slid into the seat so suddenly she almost screamed. "Asphyxia is no fun."

"How'd you sneak up on me like that?"

"Trade secret. Coast is clear."

Her nerves jumping, Rockie put the Jeep in neutral and let it roll down the tunnel. "Who are you, anyway?"

"Don't you mean what?"

"After the day I've had I'm not sure what I mean."

"Nothing's for sure but death and taxes, kid."

"I'm not a kid," Rockie snapped. "I know I look like one, but I'm not."

"Prove it."

Gravity would have stopped the Jeep at the bottom of the ramp, where the tunnel leveled out and widened into a warehouse with stainless-steel lockers built into the walls, but Rockie stomped on the brake. Hard enough to throw Maxwell forward in his seat. Hard enough to flatten his nose against the windshield, too, if he hadn't put up an arm and caught himself on the dash.

"I'm twenty-six. It says so on my driver's license."

"That's old enough to have better sense." Maxwell tucked his sunglasses in his shirt pocket and got out of the Jeep.

"Better sense than what?" Rockie opened her door and followed him.

"Better sense than to confront somebody like Conan." Maxwell turned his cap around with one hand and raked his hair back with the other as he came toward her around the nose of the Jeep. "Not to mention a dozen armed mercs."

"You saw what happened?"

"'Course I did. From up there on the hill, it would've been impossible not to."

What kind of man could just stand by and do nothing? A coldhearted SOB, Rockie reminded herself, jamming her fists on her hips to keep from punching Maxwell.

"Why didn't you *help me?*" Her voice, shrill with anger, echoed off the walls. "We might have been able to save my father from being kidnapped!"

"Or we might've both gotten our heads blown off." Maxwell snatched his gun out of its holster, so quickly Rockie backed a startled step away. "This is a nine millimeter automatic Smith & Wesson," he said, holding it under her nose. "It has fourteen rounds in a clip. An

M16 has thirty. Multiply that by twelve and figure the odds."

"You didn't like the odds so you just *watched?*"

"There was no percentage in both of us getting shot."

"So what's the percentage now, Archimedes?"

"That we'll get out of here in one piece?" Maxwell shrugged and reholstered his gun. "Depends on whether or not Conan uses those rockets to cover his tracks."

That possibility hadn't occurred to Rockie, although it should have. They weren't there for decoration. "Do you think he will?"

"Depends on his orders. You wouldn't happen to know who's giving them, would you?"

"Somebody named Smith, but that's not his real name."

"It rarely is," Maxwell said sourly.

"My father has never met him. He dealt with Smith's assistant, Greer Hanlon."

"What's the power source down here?" Maxwell moved away from her, the heels of his well-worn and dust-caked boots ringing hollowly on the concrete floor.

"Solar." Rockie watched his gaze climb the walls and track the support beams that ran alongside the duct work in the ceiling. "The storage batteries are good for twelve hours."

"If Conan didn't find them and drain them." Maxwell's gaze shifted, flicking back and forth along the length of the warehouse.

His lips weren't moving, but Rockie knew what he was doing, counting the number of reinforced steel columns connected to the support beams. He was estimating the live-load capacity, trying to figure out how many rocket hits the roof could take before it caved in. So was she.

"How much of a wallop do those rockets pack?" she asked.

"About eight thousand pounds of force per square foot."

Three Apaches, two rockets apiece. The south branch of the tunnel that led to the lab was about a mile and a half long, roughly eight thousand feet. The math was scary, the possibilities even scarier. Even if Conan shot only a couple of rockets, even if he fired them just at the lab . . .

Dry as her throat was from all the dust she'd swallowed, Rockie reached inside the Jeep for her cigarettes. She picked them up, hesitated, and glanced at Maxwell over her shoulder. He was gazing at the ceiling again, his cap pushed back on his head.

Quickly, she fished the .32 out from between the seats and slipped it in her back pocket. Then she moved away from the Jeep and lit a cigarette. Her fingers were trembling, but at least her insides had stopped shaking.

"Rockets leave tracks, too," she said.

Maxwell lowered his head and looked at her. "Cigarettes will kill you."

"So will rockets, and a helluva lot quicker." Rockie took another drag. Her fingers stopped shaking. So did her knees. "Even plastic or ceramic warheads leave chemical traces."

One corner of Maxwell's mouth lifted. "Been hanging around Daddy's lab?"

"Sometimes," Rockie said simply, deciding this was no time to trot out her credentials. "Are we just going to stand here and wait till Conan starts shooting?"

"We've got a little time. It'll take him ten or fifteen minutes to sweep the area and figure you either doubled back on him or went to ground someplace. What he'll do then is anybody's guess. He follows orders—but only to a point."

To what point, Rockie didn't want to know. She didn't want to know what Nevin Maxwell was, either. She had a pretty good idea already, enough to give her cold chills and make her wonder where and how her father had met him. Maybe she'd seen one James Bond movie too many, but she didn't think so.

She wasn't going to trust Maxwell, either, no matter what her father said. He reminded her too much of Hanlon's chauffeur. Like Conan, he was too matter-of-fact about all this. Maybe being stuck in a tunnel waiting for a rocket to fall on his head was old hat to Nevin Maxwell, but it wasn't to Rockie. She wanted out of here and away from him. She wanted badges and uniforms, things she knew she could trust.

Stepping on her cigarette, she walked around the Jeep, opened the tailgate and started filling an empty canvas backpack from the stores she'd brought along. Before Maxwell came to lean against the fender, fold his arms and watch her, she slipped the gun in an outside pocket.

"Going someplace?"

"Not at the moment." Rockie tucked a heavy-duty flashlight in the backpack and zipped it, slung a canteen she'd filled with water in L.A. over her shoulder and shut the tailgate. "This is just in case we have to make a run for it on foot."

"Smart kid." Maxwell turned his head and gazed through the tinted side window at the rest of her gear. "Looks like you came expecting trouble."

"Paranoia runs in the family. Why'd you come?"

"Because I'm out of my ever-lovin' mind."

"Why's that?"

"I'd tell you if I didn't think you'd slug me."

"What makes you so sure I would?"

"I know. Trust me."

"I don't seem to have much choice."

"Sure you do. You can wait around for Conan to make up his mind and hope to God he doesn't start shooting, or you can show me the third way out of here."

"What third way out of here?"

Maxwell unfolded his arms, moved away from the Jeep and stood gazing down at her. He was six two easy, maybe three. His eyes looked brown, but weren't. They were hazel, Rockie realized, with green-and-reddish flecks like jasper.

"Don't jerk with me, kid. We're running short on time. You don't trust me and you don't like me, any more than I trust or like you, but that gives us something in common. So does wanting to stay alive."

He turned away from her, raised his right hand and waved it around the warehouse. There were sixteen storage lockers built into the walls. Each one had its own electronic lock and number pad.

"Anybody as paranoid as your old man would've built this place around worst-case scenario. That's both exits blocked and no other way out. So I figure one of these lockers ain't a locker. It's a door." Maxwell swung back to her, his jasper eyes locked on hers. "Now, what I want to know is which one is it and what's the combination?"

Rockie ran her tongue across her sun-parched lips, but it didn't help, her mouth was dry as dust. "So far as I know, there is no third way out of here."

"Lemme explain a couple things to you." Maxwell leaned his hand on the Jeep. "One, these hills are the only ones around here for thirty miles. Conan may not have found this tunnel, but when he doesn't find your Jeep on the highway or anyplace else aboveground, he's gonna come straight back here and start looking for a cave. Most likely with a rocket. Two, he probably left at least a couple of his little windup soldiers at the lab in case you manage to double back on him. They've got more bullets than I do, so nix that way out. Three, I'd rather break your father's neck, but I'll settle for yours."

Neither his voice nor his expression changed, but Rockie knew he meant it. She saw it in his eyes. They were more red now than green or brown. Nobody had to tell her what that meant.

"I don't have a death wish," she said. "If there was another way out of this tunnel I'd tell you."

"Would you?" Maxwell folded his arms again and leaned his shoulder on the Jeep. "You wouldn't wait until the roof falls in, then whip out that little .32 peashooter you just stuck in your backpack and use it to hold me off while you waltz outta here all by your lonesome, would you?"

"Of course not. That's the kind of thing you'd do."

Rockie never saw him move. Maybe she blinked, or maybe Maxwell teleported. One second he was leaning against the Jeep, the next he had her shoulders gripped in his hands. A full five seconds before she felt the floor move and heard a low, telltale rumble. He not only had eyes in the back of his head, he had sonar for ears.

"Holy shit." He looked down at the crack spreading beneath their feet like a long-fingered bolt of lightning. "What a lousy time for an earthquake."

Rockie clung to his forearms as the tunnel groaned around them, the Jeep rocked on its springs and her memory flashed her a picture of the coffin-domed box. Rockets would leave traces, but the TAQ box wouldn't.

"I don't think it's a quake," she said to Maxwell. "I think it's the TAQ box."

He blinked, once. "Addison built it?"

"He built two. Prototypes."

"I'll kill him." Maxwell grabbed her right elbow and turned her toward the ramp. "Hit the door button."

Rockie did, fumbling the remote out of her shirt pocket. The door began to move, just as another rumble shivered past them and climbed up the ramp. One of the halide lamps exploded in a fountain of sparks. The door ground to a halt, a bare six inches of daylight showing, the steel sheeting that lined it on the inside bubbling like a balloon.

Muttering a nasty word starting with *f*, Maxwell wheeled Rockie around and towed her, stumbling and staggering as the floor quivered beneath them, toward the bank of lockers on the east wall. They'd traversed half the distance when the lights flickered twice and went out.

Over the hiss of dust sifting down on their heads, Rockie heard a loud metallic pop, then a sigh, and she froze. So did Maxwell, spinning her around to fish the flashlight out of her backpack. He switched it on and aimed it at the east wall. The lockers were slowly swinging open, a faint gap of distant, murky light showing through the fourth one.

"I'll be damned. A fail-safe system." Maxwell pulled her forward, the canteen falling off her shoulder with a *thunk*. "Maybe I won't kill your father, after all. Maybe I'll just put him in a body cast."

The floor was rippling like a wave by the time they reached the door, a low, ominous rumble groaning toward them from the south branch of the tunnel that led to the lab. Coughing in the dust billowing around her, Rockie peered down a dim metal chute that curved to the left and out of sight.

A haze of dust muted the pale light filtering up from the bottom. The chute was about four feet high and three across, its seams already grinding under stress. Rockie could hear dirt and small rocks pinging on its sheet-metal sides.

"D'you suppose it's safe?"

"It's a helluva lot safer than staying here. Ladies first."

Maxwell caught Rockie beneath her arms, lifted her off her feet and into the chute. She landed hard on her tailbone, felt the tube quivering around her and clutched the sides. She didn't like this. Oh, God, she didn't like this.

"Hang on." Maxwell swung himself in behind her and hooked his legs around hers.

"I am." Rockie squeezed her eyes shut and clung for dear life as the sides began shuddering and the seams shrieked.

"To me, not the chute." Maxwell peeled her fingers loose and clamped them on his knees.

It was enough to send them shooting down the tube into God only knew what. Maxwell locked his arms around Rockie's rib cage, and she locked her hands around his wrists just as the roof of the tunnel collapsed behind them, the roar of tons of falling concrete muffling her scream.

5

ROCKETING DOWN the chute was like dying and being born again. The metal shell amplified the roar of the cave-in billowing after them, in a cloud of dust so thick it blinded and nearly choked Rockie. Rivets popped loose and tore at her clothes. The only thing she had to cling to was Maxwell, but she lost her grip on him as they shot through the curve and out of the chute, rolling like tumbleweeds into the open onto hard, pebbled sand.

Rockie managed to suck a lungful of air before she landed on her stomach on top of her backpack and the breath slammed out of her. Dazed and aching, she lay still, straining to catch her breath and listen for the Apaches over the pounding of her heart. There was no telltale eggbeater rhythm and not so much as a groan from Maxwell, just a deadly dry rattle that froze her heart and snapped her chin up off the ground.

About eight feet in front of her, Maxwell was sprawled on his back, deadly still, eyes open. Most of the buttons had been ripped off his shirt in their plummet down the chute, exposing his dark-haired chest to the biggest rattlesnake Rockie had ever seen. It curled on a rock about a foot above him and two feet from his nose.

By the number of thick coils supporting its coffin-shaped head, she figured the snake was about twelve feet long. The grandpappy of them all, and by the irritable hiss of his rattle, royally pissed at their intrusion.

Fear and cold shivered through Rockie. The sun had sunk well below the western summit of the hills, lowering the temperature a good thirty degrees since they'd entered the tunnel. Probably the quake had brought Grandpappy out of his burrow. With any luck, the chill in the air would make him sluggish and less inclined to strike.

"Don't move," Maxwell said, his voice a hoarse, strained whisper. "You okay?"

"I think so," Rockie whispered back.

"Catch your breath. When I count three you run like—"

Maxwell broke off as the snake flicked his tongue. He knew enough to know Grandpappy was listening. So did Rockie. With her palms pressed to the ground, she felt what the snake sensed. Another tremor, hopefully an aftershock. Over the back-off-and-don't-bug-me flick of Grandpappy's rattle, she heard the Apaches.

Faint and faraway, but they were there, the timbre of their engines low and slow. Conan was on the prowl, looking for her, just like Maxwell said he would. On the other side of the hills for now, but not for long. Already the *whup-whup-whup* of their rotors was growling closer.

Close enough to irritate Grandpappy. He rattled again and flicked his tongue, his coils tightening.

"Here we go," Maxwell whispered. "One, two—"

Rockie didn't wait for three and she didn't run. She reared up on her knees and threw her backpack at Maxwell. It landed on his chest only a fraction of a second before Grandpappy struck, his fangs burying and snagging themselves in the thick, rough canvas. He writhed twice to free himself before Maxwell got his hands under the backpack and heaved it off his chest.

Then he sprang to his feet, running. So did Rockie, whirling for cover just as the first Apache came swooping over the hills, swirling dust and spitting bullets. A neatly stitched row of them exploded the dirt at Rockie's feet. Maxwell grabbed her elbow and flung her out of the way. She fell, scraping her chin on a slab of shale, but pushed up on her hands and the balls of her feet.

About thirty yards up the hill ahead of her, she saw a ledge of limestone overhanging a large jumble of boulders, and broke for it like a runner out of her blocks. The Apache shot past overhead, low enough to deafen her with the full-throttle roar of its engine, low enough to spin her around and almost flatten her in the backwash of its rotor. Maxwell grabbed her arm and kept her up and running. He nearly dislocated her shoulder, too, but she didn't have breath enough to cry out. She barely had breath enough to run.

For every two yards they gained up the slope, they lost one to the loose shingle underfoot. Treacherous as quicksand, it slid out from under them, hissing and rattling away down the hill. Over her shoulder, Rockie saw the first Apache swing around to make another pass. She also saw a thick column of black smoke, rising from the southeast where her father's lab ought to be, and a beam of late, vivid sun flashing off the Plexiglas windscreen of a second Apache diving after them.

The rapid-fire *ratta-ratta-ratta* of the gun mounted on its underbelly ripped through the shingle no more than ten yards behind them. Rockie dug in her toes; Maxwell grabbed the back of her shirt and tossed her ahead of him through the narrow cleft between the boulders. Bullets bounced off the lip of the limestone overhang, showering her with tiny, needle-sharp shards.

She landed on her stomach, hands spread to cushion the fall, what little breath she had left whooshing out of her as Maxwell rolled over her into the cleft, pushing her face first and mouth open into dank, moldy dirt. Rockie gagged and spat, raised her head and saw Maxwell draw his gun. She also saw blood trickling down his right arm.

"You're shot!" she croaked, her voice raw from all the dust she'd swallowed.

"A piece of rock winged me. A .50-caliber bullet would've blown my arm off." He crawled toward the boulders, peered over them and muttered a sharp, nasty word. "I *knew* I was out of my ever-lovin' mind."

Rockie pushed up on her hands and knees and crawled over to Maxwell. The two Apaches were setting down at the base of the slope, the slow, wind-down spin of their rotors whipping fan-blade shadows across the hard, pebbled ground. There was no sign of the third chopper.

"Where do you suppose the other one is?" Rockie asked.

"Winging Addison toward his rendezvous with Smith. Probably with Conan at the stick." Maxwell bent his right arm on the boulder and pushed his cap back with the barrel of his gun. "My guess is Conan left these guys behind to tie up the loose ends."

Rockie had been called many things in her life, a loose screw, a loose cannon, but never a loose end. It gave her a mental picture of herself dangling in midair by a piece of thread. It made her nervous and it made her mad, too, but mostly it just plain scared her.

"Are they really lousy shots," she asked, "or were we just damn lucky?"

"Those guys are excellent shots. It takes one helluva marksman to fire a .50-caliber machine gun that spits three rounds every second and *not* hit someone."

"You mean they weren't trying to kill us?"

"Not yet, or we'd be dead." Maxwell pushed his cap back another notch and scratched his temple with his gun. Rockie wished he wouldn't do that. It made her skin crawl.

"So they were just trying to scare us?"

"They were trying to scare you and run you to ground. They didn't figure on me." Maxwell looked around the narrow, shallow cleft and frowned. "They don't know who I am or what I am. I could be anybody—a hiker, a camper—but if they decide I'm the law, my ass is grass. Yours might be, too, if they think you called me, but that's doubtful."

"How doubtful?"

"Sixty you didn't, forty you did."

It wasn't a real comforting percentage. Neither was Maxwell's penchant for figuring them.

"They won't make a move until they check with Conan," he said. "That's what they're doing now, raising him on the radio."

"What do we do?"

"If you want to be reunited with dear old dad, just sit tight and wait for the soldier boys to come up the hill and collect you. Addison didn't go willingly, so my guess is this Smith character plans to use you to persuade him to cooperate." Maxwell reholstered his gun, sat back on his heels and gave the cleft a glowering but thorough inspection. "I, however, am getting the hell out of here. Just as soon as I figure out how."

"Just like that?" Rockie replied flippantly. "After all we've been to each other?"

Maxwell didn't miss her sarcasm, just like she hadn't missed his choice of pronoun and what it meant—she was on her own. Rockie prided herself on being able to handle anything, but now she knew there were things she couldn't—things like combat helicopters and mercenaries with rifles. She was dangling by a thread, all right, but she'd be damned if she'd beg for help. Especially from Maxwell.

"Listen, kid." He bent his elbows, placed his hands on his thighs and looked at her. "I don't even know your name. And frankly, that's the way I'd like to keep it."

"Fine. Then let me tell you what *I* guess," Rockie retorted. "My father was right about you. I also guess, since he tried to talk me out of coming out here, that he doesn't want me involved in this, so I guess I won't be waiting for the soldier boys to come get me or decide to shoot me. I guess I'll be getting the hell out of here, too."

It sounded childish and utterly ridiculous, even to Rockie. Where did she think she was going to go in the middle of the Mojave Desert? Nowhere that the troopers in the Apaches couldn't pluck her up at will, that's for sure.

"Be my guest." Maxwell gestured toward the narrow gap in the jumble of boulders blocking the cleft.

Rockie blinked at him, surprised. She'd expected—no, she'd hoped—he'd at least *try* to stop her. His blasé invitation stung. She didn't know why, but it did.

"I will," she said, starting to crawl toward the opening.

"Don't worry," he said behind her. "I'm 96.7 percent sure they won't shoot you."

Rockie was one hundred percent sure if she had a baseball bat she'd slug Maxwell. Gritting her teeth, she wormed her way past the boulders and scrambled up on the largest one, a two- or three-ton chunk of limestone. She no more thought the troopers would shoot her than Maxwell did. His theory, and the fact that she was still alive, made sense. Still, she was scared. Not of being shot, but of disappearing without a trace. If she let the troopers take her, would anyone besides Maxwell know what happened to her? Would anyone care?

Smoke from the burning lab still billowed into the sky, swirling into a bank of black cloud on the horizon. She had to get herself out of here and to the nearest police station ASAP, before they came to investigate the smoke and assumed her father had died in the quake. Or that she had, too.

But maybe that's what Smith wanted them to think.

The thought made Rockie shiver, but gave her courage enough to turn around on the boulder and face the Apaches. It almost gave her courage enough to stick out her tongue, but then the cockpit doors sprang open and eight troopers, four from each chopper, climbed out. Not with their guns to shoot her, just to watch her with their arms folded and grins on their faces. A pretty cocky bunch, but Rockie figured she'd be just as smug with an M16.

"Catch me if you can, boys," she muttered, steadying herself with one hand on the rock face as she turned around.

She intended to climb up the overhang, the crest of the hill just beyond it, and hopefully find a place to hide on the other side, but she paused and leaned over to take one last look and a parting shot at Maxwell. He sat watching her with a bemused smile on his face, his knees drawn up and his arms, the right one streaked with dried blood, looped around them.

"One more thing, Mr. Maxwell. I guess this means you're on your own, too."

"My name isn't Maxwell," he said. "It's Sheridan."

The boulder Rockie stood on groaned and trembled as another aftershock shivered across the slope. It was a mild jolt compared to the one shooting up her spine. She stared at the man she'd thought was Nevin Maxwell, and tried to remember where she'd heard the name Sheridan. In her father's lab, she was sure, but she couldn't recall who'd said it, why or in what context.

"Is Sheridan first or last?" she asked.

"Last. My first name's Leslie. What's yours?"

"Rockie."

"Figures. What else would a geologist name his kid?"

"It's Rochelle actually, but if you ever call me that—"

The boulder groaned again and began to tremble. So did the ground, and the edge of the overhang Rockie gripped in her hands. This was no aftershock, this was a tremor. A big one, maybe a five or six pointer. She felt the lump of limestone shift beneath her, jumped for the overhang and managed to hook her elbows over it just as the boulder heeled over and slammed into the one beside it. With an earsplitting crack, it broke the jumble of rocks blocking the cleft and sent them tumbling down the hill.

Rockie had never seen a ton of limestone bounce, and neither had Conan's troopers. She clung to the overhang, looked over her shoulder and saw their mouths fall open. The big boulder she'd been standing on only a second ago and at least a dozen others almost as big rumbled down the hillside—heading straight for the men and the grounded Apaches.

If the impact didn't explode the fuel tanks it would be a miracle. Rockie knew it and knew there wasn't time to get the choppers off the ground. The troopers knew it, too. They grabbed rifles and a field radio and ran, stumbling and falling on the ground rolling underfoot. Rockie groped for a better hold on the shivering overhang, felt Sheridan's hands close on her left ankle and glanced down at him.

"Go!" he shouted, and gave her a boost that sent her shooting over the edge.

Rockie tucked, rolled and came up on her feet, off-balance and wobbling, but on her feet. The entire hillside was heaving, the ground rippling. Sheridan swung himself up behind her, caught her arm and pulled her with him over the crest of the hill.

They made it halfway down the sandy slope on the other side before the fuel tanks blew. The concussion nearly deafened Rockie. Only Sheridan's hand on her arm kept her up and moving. Fire crackled in her ears, a shrill whistle cut through the ringing in her head. At the base of the slope, she slid to a stop beside Sheridan, glanced back, and saw several chunks of flaming debris sailing over the hill. One plopped into the sand a few yards behind them, a piece of twisted, charred rotor.

"That evens the odds some," Sheridan said, pulling her forward again.

They ran until the roar of the fire faded to a dull hiss behind them, until Rockie wasn't sure if the shudder she felt with every step was in the ground or in her knees, until they reached a small outcrop of rock casting long purple shadows on the sandy desert floor. When Sheridan let go of her arm, she leaned over, wrapped her hands above her knees and breathed, blinking back the spots swimming in her vision. Every inch of her ached, her throat was raw and throbbing, but at least she was alive. She wondered about Conan's troopers, but didn't look back to see until Sheridan led her into the rocks and they'd hunkered down behind a pie-shaped slab of sandstone.

Smoke still poured over the crest of the hill about a mile away, but no troopers. Rockie shivered in the chill creeping into the air and rubbed her arms.

"S'pose any of them survived?" she asked Sheridan.

"Dunno." He drew his gun and leaned it against the slab in his right hand. "But we're gonna make sure."

Make sure they did, or make sure they didn't? Rockie wondered, but didn't ask. She leaned against the sandstone slab and closed her eyes. She kept them closed until she heard—something—that sent a chill up her back. She didn't recognize it as a chopper until she sprang up on her knees and saw the flash of a whipping rotor rising over the hill. Her first thought was Conan, her second was run, until Sheridan trapped her elbow in his hand.

"Hang on a minute," he said. "Don't you want to meet Maxwell?"

6

THAT'S EXACTLY what she was doing, Sheridan realized as she turned her head and looked at him. Hanging on. Barely, by a thread, a thin and badly frayed one.

He read it in her eyes. They were green as grass and glassy as emeralds. She blinked and looked away from him, at the sleek, almost silent chopper skimming over the hill, then back at him, and wrenched her elbow out of his grasp.

"I've never seen anything like that except in a science fiction movie," she said. "How d'you know it's Maxwell?"

A moment ago, her pupils had been huge with panic. Now they were contracted, her eyes narrow with suspicion.

"'Cause I work for him sometimes." Sheridan tucked his gun away and stood up. "And I've flown the Raptor."

Of course, it had only been once—and almost into the side of a butte. Max had nearly had heart failure. Not from the close one with the butte, but the close one with God only knew how many millions the turbojet chopper had cost him. The memory made Sheridan's palms sweat and his pulse quicken. He never thought he'd get this close to the Raptor again, not after Max had red-tagged his file. A scary guy, Max.

Wexler's daughter sprang up beside him. "What do you mean you only work for him *sometimes?*"

"'Cause the rest of the time I do something else," Sheridan replied as he climbed up on the sandstone slab.

"Like *what?*"

"Whatever I damn well feel like," he snapped, waving his arms over his head.

He didn't blame her for being wary and distrustful. He resented it, but he didn't blame her. Distrust and suspicion were old friends of his, who dropped in for frequent visits. Especially at the mention of anything or anyone pertaining to Addison Wexler.

"Oh, I see." She threw her weight, what little there was of it, on her left hip and cocked her head to the side. "So you're just a dilettante."

"Nope. I'm a pain in the ass."

Maxwell must have seen him; the Raptor banked out of its search sweep and veered toward him. Sheridan jumped off the slab and looked at Wexler's daughter. "Ask anybody who knows me. Ask Max. Or your father the next time you see him."

"If I ever do, I will."

"Don't worry. You'll see him. Guys like Addison Wexler always land on their feet." Sheridan moved away from the slab and watched the Raptor approach, a fading ray of twilight sun winking on the fluted turbo vents in her trim, blue-gray hull. "Somebody always has to grab 'em by the scruff of the neck and haul 'em up so they don't fall on their face, but they never seem to notice that."

Over the whine of the Raptor's jet turbine, he heard the bitterness in his voice and felt surprise. Addison

Wexler was a lying, thieving egomaniac who used people like toilet paper, but he'd gotten over that a long time ago. At least Sheridan thought he had, but he felt another surge of it, like bile in the back of his throat, as Wexler's daughter rounded the slab and stood in front of him. Close, but not so close that she had to raise her head to look him in the eye.

"You've done that before, haven't you? Hauled my father up by the scruff of his neck."

She was a sharp kid. Prickly, too, like her old man.

"A time or two." He looked away from her to watch the Raptor land, smooth as silk on landing gear rather than talons, but just as swift, just as deadly, and almost as silent as the winged predators Maxwell had named it for.

"Is that why you came this time?"

"No." Sheridan pulled his gaze away from the Raptor and let it settle on Wexler's daughter. She was filthy, but he imagined he was, too. She had sand and dirt matted in her hair and her eyebrows, a dozen or more scratches and dried blood on her chin. "This time I came to wring his neck."

He hadn't intended to come at all. He still wasn't sure why he had. Curiosity, maybe, or the chance to gloat, but the existence of the TAQ box had changed all that. She had a right to know. Up front. So there wouldn't be any misunderstandings later.

"Addison Wexler is my father," she said, like he could forget. "I came to *save* his neck."

"Then you should have gone with Conan and his boys."

She flinched, but didn't look away. Sheridan wished she would. It was the truth, but she didn't need to hear it, any more than he needed to feel guilty for saying it.

"No matter what you think my father wouldn't want that. He'd never allow it. Not even to save his life."

She spun away from him on one foot and started toward the Raptor. A tricorner tear in the back of her shirt showed a thin white bra strap and a shapely shoulder blade. That's another thing he couldn't forget, his first good look at her when she'd bailed out of the Jeep. He was out of his mind, all right, absolutely out of his ever-lovin' mind to feel anything for anybody named Wexler. Even sympathy.

When the cockpit door opened and Maxwell got out, she stopped cold in her tracks. Sheridan didn't need to see her face to know she was staring. Probably with her mouth open. Max always had that effect on women, until they looked in his eyes. Wexler's daughter raised her fingers to the wind-snarled black curls tangled around her face. When her hand froze, Sheridan figured she'd made eye contact. The shiver that rippled across her exposed shoulder blade confirmed it.

"Miss Wexler." Maxwell stepped away from the Raptor and offered his hand. "Nevin Maxwell."

"Hello." She moved to shake his hand, but abruptly drew her arm back, rubbed her palm on her jeans to emphasize how dirty it was, and tucked it in her back pocket.

The snub went right over his head. It always did, poor bastard. Because he'd known Maxwell for eight years, Sheridan knew his cobalt blue eyes hadn't always been so dead and lifeless. He knew why, too.

"Anybody make it back there?" he asked.

Maxwell lifted his gaze from Rockie Wexler and gave a single shake of his head. Sheridan glanced at the fuel fire still blackening the sky beyond the hill. Wexler's kid was looking, too, staring tight jawed at the thin trail of smoke beginning to dissipate above her old man's lab.

"How's your arm?" Maxwell asked.

"Just a scratch." Sheridan shrugged and walked toward him. When he stopped next to Wexler's daughter, she moved away, chafing her folded arms. "Sure wish you and your new toy had been here about an hour ago."

"What happened?"

"An earthquake. It took out those two Apaches. There's another one with .50 caliber gun and a launcher full of rockets floating around here someplace. Wexler's aboard with a few more mercs and your buddy Conan."

Maxwell was watching Rockie Wexler watch the smoke, but he swung his gaze back to Sheridan when he said the name Conan. "Are you sure it was him?"

"Positive. Matched the ID on the hot sheet you put out on him last year to a *T*." Sheridan unbuttoned his shirt pocket and fished out the cigarettes and disposable lighter he'd filched from the backpack before the tunnel roof caved in. "Hey, kid."

She glanced at him over her shoulder, her lashes wet, but her face still dirty and untracked. She caught the badly crumpled pack he tossed her but missed the lighter, picked it up and shot him a grateful smile.

"Thanks. I think I could kiss—" She bit her tongue. "Never mind. No, I couldn't. Not even for a cigarette."

Sheridan would have kissed Conan for a cigarette, but didn't say so. As she lit up he edged closer and sucked a lungful of secondhand smoke. His nostrils flared and his mouth watered, but he managed not to whimper when she moved farther away and stood with her back to him. Just his luck she was one of those mindful-of-offending-others smokers, but at least she'd moved out of earshot.

"I thought you'd quit smoking," Maxwell said.

"This job could get me started again."

"You said you weren't interested. What changed your mind?"

"The TAQ box. Wexler built it."

There wasn't so much as a flicker, of surprise or anything else, in Maxwell's eyes. "Is that what started the quake?"

"She says so. God knows it wouldn't take much to start one in these parts. California has more faults than I do."

"Is there a way to find out?"

"Might be something at the lab, if there's anything left of it. There's a couple more things you should know. The mercs in the Apaches could have made mincemeat out of us. They didn't. Addison left his lab at gunpoint. Conan's working for a guy using the name Smith. I think he'd like to get his hands on the kid over there, use her to make sure Addison cooperates."

Maxwell thought about it, for all of two seconds. "In that case, I think we should be going. Miss Wexler, we're leaving now."

"I'm not going anywhere until I get a straight answer to a straight question," she said as she turned around. This time there were tracks on her cheeks. "Do you intend to help me find my father?"

"That's why I'm here."

"Thank Go— I mean, great. I wasn't sure how I was going to explain all this to the cops." She dropped her gaze along with her cigarette. The deep breath she drew and exhaled stopped the quaver in her chin. "Where are we going?"

"First, to see if there's anything left of the lab," Maxwell replied, "anything that might give us a clue to what happened to your father, who took him and why."

"He was kidnapped by a guy named Smith, who was funding his research on the TAQ box. Dad never met him, but he knew that wasn't his real name. His contact with Smith is a guy named Greer Hanlon. I've never met him, but I saw him once."

"Tell me more." Maxwell gestured toward the Raptor. "But tell me on the way, Miss Wexler."

"Call me Rockie, please."

"Rockie it is. Call me Max."

"Okay, Max."

He gave her a curt, atta-girl nod and turned toward the Raptor. She trailed after him, smiling and tugging at the snarls in her hair again.

Sheridan rolled his eyes and followed.

7

UNTIL HE'D LOST his pilot's license in a flap with the FAA, Addison Wexler had owned a helicopter. He'd used it for hops to the marine base at Twenty-One Palms where he sometimes did research and development, and to ferry Rockie back and forth to L.A. As a result she thought she was an old hand at choppers, until she belted herself into the seat behind Sheridan, cupping the headset he handed her over her ears, and Maxwell eased back on the stick and the collective.

One second the Raptor was on the ground, the next it was airborne and streaking—or so it seemed to Rockie—like a comet toward the lab. There wasn't much engine noise and little vibration. What she could see of the control panel between the forward seats reminded her of the navigation console on the USS *Enterprise*—the one in the United Federation of Planets, not the U.S. Navy.

So she hadn't seen one James Bond movie too many, after all, Rockie thought. When the Raptor skimmed over the ring of half-moon hills behind her father's lab, she wanted to scream and cuss when she saw how little was left of it.

The garage and smaller sheds had been flattened, the data-storage building and her father's house were blackened heaps of rubble. A few small fires still smoldered in the yard, and smoke—or maybe steam—

curled from a fissure in the parking lot. The main lab was the only structure that had survived; if by survived you meant a cracked and bowed north wall, shattered windows and half the roof gone.

Rockie called it a declaration of war. Her father's lifework was down there. So were her mother's things, all but the few mementos she'd kept in her apartment in L.A. It was all a shambles now, a complete ruin. Maybe she couldn't handle combat choppers and mercenaries—not yet, anyway—but she'd learn. And she was a damn quick study. She'd find her father first, then she'd find Smith and make him pay for this.

"Doesn't look like there's much point setting down," Maxwell's voice was clear as a bell in Rockie's headset as he piloted the Raptor through a second loop around the compound. "Not without a bulldozer."

"We're here, we might as well," Sheridan replied. "Hey, kid. Where am I most likely to find anything pertinent that Conan might've missed?"

"My name isn't *kid,*" Rockie snapped, blinking back hot, angry tears. "And don't worry, I'll show you."

"The hell you will."

"The hell I *will* if you want to find it."

Sheridan popped his head between the seats. His jasper eyes were mostly green, his dark hair sticking out in dirt-stiffened spikes around his headset. He'd lost his Cubs hat, Rockie realized, someplace between the snake and the quake. She couldn't remember when, where or how, a sure sign of sensory overload. So was the glare on Sheridan's face.

"You aren't qualified to go into a quake-damaged structure," he said. "I am."

"Oh, really?" Rockie asked sweetly. "What are you? A looter as well as a pain in the ass?"

Maxwell laughed. Sheridan glowered. Rockie glowered back. She'd had enough for one day. Enough of being shot at, chased by helicopters, shaken until her teeth rattled and bullied by a man she didn't even know. A man who knew but didn't like her father. Maybe he had good reason, but she was through taking abuse for it.

"I'm a structural engineer," Sheridan replied curtly.

"Bully for you, but unless you also happen to be clairvoyant, you haven't a prayer of finding my father's hiding places. I, however, know exactly where to look, and I can show you a heck of a lot easier than I can tell you."

"She's got a point," Maxwell said, before Sheridan could open his mouth.

"You're the boss." He straightened in his seat and snapped off his safety harness. "Gimme a minute to check and make sure what's left of the roof isn't gonna come down on our heads."

"One minute," Maxwell said firmly, setting the Raptor down a dozen or so yards from the lab. "Where's your transport, by the way?"

"About thirty yards up in those hills." Sheridan clipped a battery pack to his belt and plugged his headset into it. "Rented dune buggy."

"I'll take care of it. We don't want to leave any loose ends."

"Thanks. Wait here, kid." Sheridan kicked open the door and bailed out of the cockpit.

"Fat chance," Rockie muttered. She was out of her harness and headset and halfway out of the Raptor behind Sheridan before Maxwell caught her elbow.

"Sherry knows what he's doing," he said, when she glanced at him over her shoulder. "He has a doctorate in structural engineering, one in geology and another in seismology."

Rockie blinked, surprised. Sheridan didn't look like any brainiac she'd ever met, and she'd spent a good portion of her life in the company of rocket scientists. He looked like what he was, a pain in the ass. Rockie had met more than a few of those in Hollywood.

"How old was he when he started college? Fourteen?"

"Twelve, actually."

Rockie blinked again. Maxwell smiled.

"He also has a masters in Medieval-French literature. Unfortunately, he flunked social interaction."

"Who cares. Can he cook?"

Maxwell grinned. It almost, but not quite, reached his eyes. "Only in a laboratory."

Rockie could have graduated high school at fifteen, if her parents had let her. They hadn't. Now she knew why. She also had an idea why Sheridan so obviously disliked her father. Scientific birds did not flock together. More often than not, they pecked each other to death.

She glanced thoughtfully toward the lab just as Sheridan stepped into the blown-out doorway and signaled to her. She still had no idea when or where he'd met her father, or how someone with his credentials had ended up working for Maxwell. Even sometimes.

"Go," Maxwell said to her. "Five minutes, Sherry," he said into his headset.

Sheridan nodded and Rockie went, ducking the rotor and running. Behind her, the Raptor wheeled into the air. On the ground it was a sitting duck, especially if Conan was still lurking in the third Apache. The thought gave her a chill, as she hurried up the steps. Broken glass crunched under her feet.

"Where's Addison's office?" Sheridan asked, taking her arm as she came through the doorway.

"Second floor, next to the lab," she replied numbly as she glanced around the foyer.

Slabs of superreinforced walls, designed to withstand an eight-point earthquake, lay like toppled monoliths across the buckled and fissured floor. Water from the sprinkler system dripped from the ceiling, pooling into small lakes in places where the tiles had sunk. The last time Rockie had been in the lab and a four-point tremor had rolled across the Mojave, the building hadn't so much as quivered. Now it groaned around her like a thing in pain.

So did the main staircase, listing at a drunken angle away from the wall in front of her. Its stainless-steel banister was gone in some places and hanging by shreds in others. It looked like the only thing holding it up was air.

"It'll support us if we go up one at a time." Sheridan tugged her out of her daze toward the rubble-strewn staircase. "You first. Wait for me at the top."

Just this once, Rockie decided not to argue with him. She nodded, took a deep breath and started up, the steps creaking and the landing quivering beneath her. When she could find one, she grasped a solid length of banister and used it to lever herself past a chunk of wall or ceiling.

Her hands, white knuckled and clammy on the rail, reminded her of the first time she'd seen the TAQ box, of tapping her finger on the power knob. She could almost see Conan's big hand and blunt-tipped fingers twisting it as far as it would go. The memory made her shiver and rub her arms as she reached the second floor and Sheridan climbed up behind her, the steps groaning under him.

"Let's move," he said, taking her elbow again as she led him into the lab.

Most of the roof lay on the floor, and smoke drifted in the fading sunlight slanting through the gaps. Water dripped from everything, including what was left of the ceiling.

"Hang on a minute," Sheridan said, letting go of her.

He picked his way across the debris-strewn lab, pushed a capsized steel storage cabinet off the seismograph, blew dust off the printout tape curling out of it and tore off as much as the ruined machine would let go of. He folded it and tucked it inside his shirt, fastened the only two buttons he had left and nodded her toward her father's office.

The carpet was soaked and squished underfoot; the surface of the oak desk had already warped. The PC monitor linked to the mainframe in the lab flashed. Rockie ignored it, but Sheridan didn't.

"'If you're reading this, Smith, you're too late.'" He read the message blinking on the blue screen, then looked up at Rockie. "Looks like Addison knew Conan was on his way."

"I got that impression on the phone," she replied, searching the right-hand desk drawer for the TV/VCR remote control.

She found it under a rubber-banded stack of ten-year-old bank statements and breathed a sigh of relief that it wasn't soaked. The twenty-five-inch color TV and the VCR were melted lumps of plastic and components on the wall shelves across the room. Rockie turned her back on them and pressed the Pause and Fast Forward buttons on the remote simultaneously.

The tiny transmitter her father had built into it tripped a fake board in the oak paneling. It should have popped gently open; instead, it shot out of the wall on a tongue of flame. If Sheridan hadn't ducked, it would have taken his left ear off along with his headset. The board whistled past him and landed with a plop, hissing and steaming, in a puddle a good six feet in front of the desk.

Sheridan scooped his dripping headset off the floor, shook it and eyed the lead-lined, air- and watertight box attached to the board dubiously. Then he eyed Rockie, suspiciously.

"Cute trick. Got any more up your sleeve?"

"Got any Thorazine you can take for your whopping case of paranoia?" Rockie rounded the desk and used the filthy tails of her denim shirt like pot holders to pick up the box.

"This ain't paranoia, kid. This is the voice of experience."

Bitter experience, by the edge in his voice. With life in general, Rockie wondered, or her father in particular?

The box was hot, but not as hot as it would have been if it hadn't landed in the puddle. Her fingertips tingling from the heat, Rockie carried it to the desk. Sheridan swept the soaked blotter aside and spread a water-spotted but mostly dry computer printout. Rockie put the box down, pressed the Mute key on the remote and the lid popped open.

"Well, well," Sheridan said dryly. "You're just full of little secrets, aren't you?"

"You keep getting me confused with my father, Sheridan." Rockie used her shirttails to grasp the box again. "I'm Rockie. Addison is the Wexler with the mustache."

"Ever thought of growing one? Might look good on you."

"Ever thought about knocking that chip off your shoulder?" She emptied the box on the blotter and nodded at the half-dozen 2MG hard plastic computer disks that tumbled onto the printout. "If Dad left a written record of his dealings with Smith, he left it here. These are his diary disks."

Rockie tossed the box aside and reached for the disks. So did Sheridan, yanking them out of her grasp and tucking them in his shirt pocket. Rockie's fingertips still burned, and so did her cheeks as she watched him button the flap over the disks.

"You're welcome," she snapped.

"Let's go," he replied curtly, coming toward her around the desk and reaching for her arm again.

This time Rockie jerked away from him. "If I didn't intend to give you those disks, why d'you think I insisted on coming with you so you'd be sure to find them?"

"You don't want to know what I think."

"Then why do you keep telling me?"

"'Cause you keep asking." Sheridan caught her elbow and shoved her ahead of him through the door.

Rockie spun back to confront him, but her left foot was on sodden rug, her right on tile that was bare, wet and slick as ice. Her foot shot out from under her and she fell, hard, hydroplaning halfway across the lab on her tush. The corner of a stainless-steel lab table severed by a section of roof stopped her with a nasty crack on the back of her skull.

Rockie saw stars and shook her head. She almost expected to hear Sheridan laughing at her, but didn't. All she heard was his footsteps splashing toward her and an odd ticking sound coming from under the broken table.

"You okay?"

"Just peachy," Rockie snapped, her head and her tailbone throbbing as she struggled up on all fours and poked her head under the table.

One of the TAQ box prototypes blinked back at her, its systems diagnostics and function lights winking like little red-and-yellow spider's eyes. Rockie's heart and her voice froze in her throat as she realized the ticking wasn't coming from the TAQ box. It was coming from the bomb, the big fat one wired into its control panel, the detonator counting backward from seven minutes in red digital numbers.

"Whataya got?" One of Sheridan's knees popped as he dropped to his heels beside her. "Oh, shit. A present from Conan."

"He shouldn't have. Really," Rockie said shakily. "Tell me you can defuse it."

"In my dreams, maybe. Explosives are our friend Conan's signature, his trademark. He's an expert, a screaming genius."

Screaming sounded like a real good plan to Rockie, but instead, she asked, "What're we gonna do?"

"Run like hell." Sheridan grabbed the collar of her shirt and hauled her to her feet. "As far and as fast as we can in six minutes and forty-seven seconds."

8

ROCKIE DIDN'T ASK how far he thought they'd get. She figured she'd find out soon enough. The instant her feet touched the floor, she bolted for the doorway, caught the frame with her fingers and used it to slingshot herself into the hallway.

"We got trouble, Max," Sheridan said behind her. "More plastique than I've ever seen due to blow in—Max? Yo, Max, talk to me."

Rockie flung a look at Sheridan over her shoulder as she raced for the stairs. He was frowning, and the headset cupped to his ear dripped water on the grimy front of his shirt.

"Shorted out." He dropped the headset around his neck and took her arm as they reached the steps. "You first. Stick to the inside. I'll be right behind you."

Rockie went, hugging the wall. Sheridan started down behind her as the wall groaned. Was it joint stress or another tremor? she wondered, counting fifteen seconds since they'd left the lab. When she reached the turn in the staircase and stepped onto the landing, it tipped, tilted and shuddered beneath her.

Rockie froze, eyes shut, heart banging.

"Aftershock," Sheridan said behind her. "Wait'll it passes."

Rockie did, counting six more seconds before the landing stopped quivering.

"One at a time from here. Take this. And the battery pack." Sheridan turned her around and draped the headset around her shoulders. "Just in case."

"In case what?" Rockie asked, gooseflesh tracking the water dripping down her collar.

"Don't be stupid." Sheridan unsnapped the battery pack from his belt and clipped it over hers. "Just go."

"Not without you."

The fierceness in Rockie's voice surprised her. Sheridan, too. She saw it in the sharp, sideways jerk of his chin, felt it in the rough tug on her belt.

"Don't gimme any lip." He plucked the disks from his shirt pocket and stuffed them into hers. "Just go."

He shoved her, hard, and sent her stumbling across the landing. It groaned beneath her, shooting a shiver up her back as she grabbed the rail and flew down the last ten steps. Her right foot no sooner hit terra semi-firma when another groan rumbled up the stairwell.

Rockie had never heard a steel I-beam snap before, but knew that's what the splintering crack was behind her. She knew, too, that Sheridan hadn't a prayer of making it off the staircase—and that he must've known it when he gave her the headset and the disks.

"Jump!" she shouted, spinning toward him on one foot.

Sheridan did, arms outflung like Superman, as the steps collapsed in a grinding, shrieking roar. Rockie leapt to catch him, locking her hands on his wrists and hooking her right leg around a chunk of fallen wall. If she hadn't, the drag of his weight as he slammed into the side of the stairwell shaft would have pulled her over the edge.

He clung to her and the lip of the forty-foot drop, scrabbling for a foothold, the muscles and tendons in his arms and neck bulging. Smoke and dust billowed out of the shaft, choking him and blinding Rockie. She clenched her jaw and threw back her head, as much to keep from screaming at the tearing wrench on her arms as to hang on to Sheridan.

"Let go," he gasped. "You aren't strong enough."

"No!" He was slipping away from her, but she couldn't—she *wouldn't*—let go. "C'mon, Sheridan! Wexlers never quit. What's your problem?"

His chin shot up and he glared at her. He was breathing hard, with a sharp, shallow catch that smacked of pain. His face was ashen beneath an inch or so of dirt and dark whiskers; his wrists were slick with sweat and grit. Grabbing fistfuls of his shirt, Rockie yanked with all her might. She meant to haul him over the edge, but only managed to rip one seam and pull him nose to nose with her.

"Give it up and get outta here," he panted breathlessly.

"The hell I will."

"You're an even bigger pain in the ass than I am," he said raggedly. "I like that in a woman."

Then he kissed her. Awkwardly, off center and mostly on her teeth, as she clenched for another try at pulling him out of the shaft. Rockie's eyes sprang wide with surprise at the kiss—and the hand that snaked suddenly out of the air and clamped around Sheridan's wrists. The same big hand she'd last seen reaching through the window of her Jeep.

"Allow me," Conan said.

With a startled yelp, Rockie threw herself back on her hands as he lifted Sheridan out of the shaft. Effortlessly, as if he weighed no more than she did. Then he stepped back and wrapped one hand loosely around the grip of the Uzi slung over his shoulder.

Rockie imagined she was as ripped, torn and filthy as Sheridan, yet Conan's hands were clean and his fatigues still neatly creased. Did the guy use Scotchgard instead of deodorant?

"Thanks. I think." Sheridan straightened, left hand pressed to his ribs, an audible catch in his breathing.

"You're welcome, Dr. Sheridan."

"How d'you know my name?"

"Please. As you said to Miss Wexler, don't be stupid."

Uh-oh. He'd seen and heard everything. Rockie had no idea where he'd come from or how long he'd been here, but she knew why—the disks in her shirt pocket. She crept backward toward the door like a crab, the headset crackling around her neck.

"That's far enough, Miss Wexler." Conan glanced at her and motioned her toward Sheridan with the Uzi. "Over here, please. You have a choice to make."

Rockie hesitated, counting seconds. She'd lost track of how many had ticked by, but figured it was close to two minutes. Now she wondered how many to the door, how many for Conan to draw a bead on her. How many—

"You'll never make it," he said, as if he could read her mind. "I wouldn't enjoy shooting you, but I will."

Rockie believed him, got up and walked toward Sheridan. She kept her head down, watching the connection and channel lights on the battery pack flicker as the headset spat another burst of static. Either Conan didn't see it or didn't care. Sheridan saw, she was sure; when she stopped beside him, he stepped half in front of her.

"One moment." From the pocket of his fatigue shirt, Conan withdrew a transmitter and pressed it with his thumb. "I've stopped the countdown on the device in the laboratory at three minutes and twelve seconds. Now we have all the time in the world."

He smiled as he dropped the transmitter back in his pocket. Rockie shivered. Maybe Conan had all the time in the world, but she and Sheridan had no more than he chose to give them. Since the bomb had been ticking when they'd found it, she figured Conan hadn't arrived much before he'd pulled Sheridan out of the shaft. Hopefully, he hadn't seen the Raptor. Hopefully, he thought they were alone.

Two minutes and thirty-five seconds had elapsed, which meant the five minutes Maxwell had given them ought to be about up. Please, God, he was on his way back to retrieve them. Please, God, the static bursts from the headset meant it was drying rather than dying. And please, God, Maxwell could hear what was happening.

"You have two options, Miss Wexler," Conan said. "You can give me the disks and Dr. Sheridan, or you can keep them and come with me yourself."

"Sheridan?" Rockie blinked, startled. "What's he got to do with this?"

"Don't ask stupid questions." Sheridan swung toward her and made a grab at her pocket. "Just gimme the disks."

"No." Rockie slapped her hand over her chest and skittered out of his reach. "Why does he want you?"

"What difference does it make?" Sheridan scowled at her, the cuts and scrapes bleeding on his chest already starting to bruise. "Gimme the disks and get outta here."

"Like I'm so *sure*," Rockie retorted, "he's going to let one of us go."

"I'm a businessman, Miss Wexler, not a liar," Conan said. "I said I'd release one of you, and I will. But *only* one of you. If you choose not to accompany me and your father still refuses to cooperate with my employer, Dr. Sheridan's knowledge of the TAQ box will be invaluable."

"*What* knowledge of the TAQ box?" Rockie demanded of Sheridan. He didn't answer, just clamped his mouth shut and looked away from her, a muscle working in his jaw.

"Your father didn't tell you?" Conan said. "Dr. Sheridan invented the TAQ box. Dr. Wexler stole it from him."

This was almost as big a jolt as the quake that had flattened her Jeep. So was the sudden, vivid flash of recall that shot through Rockie's brain. She remembered now exactly where and when she'd heard Sheridan's name. Whispered between two of her father's assistants, Jennifer Phillips and Rodney Webster, over a table piled with components. Bits and pieces of the TAQ box, Rockie knew now but hadn't known then.

"I met Sheridan at a symposium on quake detection," Jennifer said. "He abandoned his research on the TAQ box when it proved as unstable as the San Andreas Fault."

"Sheridan isn't an egomaniac," Rodney replied. "He's a responsible scientist, which is more than I can say for Wexler."

"We can't let him build this thing, Rod. Sheridan used to work for Wexler. He said—"

"*Used* to, Jen. We work for him now. Don't bite the hand that signs your paycheck."

An out-of-context conversation wasn't proof positive, neither was anything Conan said, but the expression on Sheridan's face was. He closed his eyes, a ruddy flush blotching his throat. When he opened them, his right hand closed into a fist as he spun on Conan. The I'll-kill-you flash Rockie saw in his jasper eyes made her heart turn over.

"Thanks for stealing my thunder. If I wasn't ninety-three percent certain I'd puncture a lung," he said raspily, "I'd knock your goddamn teeth down your throat."

"Live dangerously, Dr. Sheridan. There's a seven percent chance you won't."

"You're not worth it."

Conan's smile widened, the nose of the Uzi swung toward Rockie. She jumped a startled step back and felt her left heel slip off the edge of the shaft. She leapt clear, heart pounding in her throat, an idea springing in her head.

"Never mind, Miss Wexler. I'll decide. Since I seriously doubt Dr. Sheridan would ever cooperate, I choose you."

"You got that right." Sheridan coughed, winced and bent double gasping for breath, one hand wrapped around his leg just above the knee, the other clutching his side.

"You don't need either one of us," Rockie said. "You've got the second prototype. Just dismantle it."

"I thought of that. So did Dr. Wexler. He installed a self-destruct mechanism. Without the schematic, you have exactly three seconds once the case is removed to disarm it."

He didn't say if the schematic was anywhere it had to be on the disks, but he didn't have to. Her own common sense told her. So did the look Sheridan gave her as he straightened, slowly, his face chalky.

"Here." Rockie fished the disks out of her pocket. "They're yours. Take them."

"If it were up to me, Miss Wexler, I'd accept them gladly and be gone, but my employer believes in insurance." Conan gestured Sheridan toward the shaft with the Uzi. "As you were, please, Doctor."

"Let him go or I'll drop these." Rockie held the disks over the edge. "I swear to God I will."

Conan turned his head and looked at her. What little daylight was left found its way through a gap in the roof and gleamed on his broad forehead. His perpetual smile was gone, the bones of his skull strong and pronounced as a helmet.

"Take a good look around, Miss Wexler. This is a small example of what happens to people who cross my employer. You're risking your life—and your father's."

"My father risked his life when he took Smith's money," Rockie replied shakily. "Maybe he didn't realize it until it was too late, but when he did, he took every precaution he could think of—or had time for—to keep Smith from getting his hands on these disks. He left them for me, so it's *my* choice what happens to them. I choose not to give them to you or anybody else who intends to use the TAQ box for destruction. That's not its purpose."

"But of course it is, Miss Wexler." Conan's smile came back. "And your father knew it."

"Give it up," Rockie jeered, with all the bravado she could muster. "You can't rattle me with your lies or scare me with that Uzi. I'm already afraid. You can't scare me any more."

"Can't I?" Conan took the transmitter out of his pocket and held his thumb over the switch. "With broken ribs, I doubt Dr. Sheridan can pull himself out of the shaft in three minutes and twelve seconds. Be sensible, Miss Wexler. Put the disks in your pocket and I'll let him walk out of here."

"Don't do it," Sheridan said. "Drop 'em."

"Drop them," Conan put in quickly, "and I'll shoot him."

"Shoot him and I *will* drop them," Rockie threatened.

Then she held her breath, terrified that Conan would lose his temper or his patience and shoot them both. Why he hadn't already, she couldn't fathom.

There was heat in the smoke drifting up from the bottom of the shaft, and an overbright glitter in Sheridan's eyes. Rockie hoped it wasn't just pain and the beginnings of shock. She prayed it was the gleam of some brilliant, last-ditch plan to save their necks, but she was afraid it wasn't, afraid she was only imagining the vibration she felt more than heard. It seeped up her bones from the floor, set her teeth on edge and her heart banging.

It wasn't real, it couldn't be real. Sheridan would hear it. So would Conan. He'd swing that Uzi around so fast—

Which he did, almost as Rockie thought it, so suddenly she jumped and almost dropped the disks. On one foot Conan spun toward the blown-out doorway, just as the Raptor dropped into view, hovering outside beyond the cracked and broken steps like a giant wasp, grit and ground-up glass swirling around its landing gear.

"Let's see if I can scare *you* now," Maxwell said over the Raptor's external speakers. "What's your preference? A rocket in the gut or a .50-caliber bullet between the eyes?"

"Nevin Maxwell, I presume?" Conan asked, sliding his thumb over the transmitter switch.

"At your service. And you are—?"

"That's what everyone asks me," Conan replied, a chuckle in his voice.

If he noticed Rockie sliding the disks into her pocket and dropping to her heels, he gave no sign. Still, she held her breath as she groped for a chunk of broken wall. She meant to throw it at him, but Sheridan was quicker. The back kick he aimed at Conan caught him in the chest, knocked the Uzi out of his hand, but not the transmitter.

The gun clattered, spinning, onto the wet, buckled floor. Rockie dived for it, slicing her chin open on a ragged piece of tile. She barely felt it, came up with the Uzi and scrabbled onto her tailbone, fumbling for the trigger. Sheridan threw another kick, Conan grabbed his ankle and tossed him aside.

Sheridan managed to get his hands under him as he fell; still he landed hard on his chest with a *whump* that knocked what little breath he had out of him. Barely winded, Conan wheeled toward Rockie. With shaking fingers, she raised the Uzi and pointed it at him. He held the transmitter high in his left hand so neither she nor Maxwell could miss seeing it.

"The safety is off, Miss Wexler. Just squeeze the trigger."

Rockie hooked her finger around it, braced herself for the kick, but couldn't do it. He'd kidnapped her father, had come back to finish destroying the lab, and still she couldn't shoot him.

Sheridan groaned, shook his head and tried to push himself up. Conan glanced at him, at the Raptor setting down outside the lab, then settled his gaze on Rockie.

"Better hurry, Miss Wexler. Only three minutes and twelve seconds."

Then he smiled at her, pressed the switch on the transmitter and leapt over the edge into the shaft.

9

IT WAS CONAN'S SMILE that haunted Rockie. Not Sheridan's bring-up-your-lungs cough, not the aftershock that rippled the floor when she and Maxwell hauled him to his feet and into the Raptor, not even the colossal explosion that shook the chopper two minutes, six seconds and eight miles after takeoff.

She told herself it was nicotine withdrawal that kept her nerves jangling long after the emergency room doctor admitted Sheridan for X rays and observation and closed the gash in her chin with four stitches. But when Maxwell checked them into adjoining rooms in the poshest hotel in Barstow and she sank into the Jacuzzi, exhausted and aching, it was Conan's smile she saw when she closed her eyes.

She still couldn't put a name to the flicker she'd seen in his eyes before he'd leapt into the shaft, but she saw a glimpse of it in Sheridan's jasper eyes when she stepped into his private hospital room at eleven o'clock the next morning. It was there for just a second as he turned his head on stark white pillows, saw her and started to smile.

Then he remembered who she was, scowled and said, "Go away. I'm dying."

"Don't make promises you can't keep." Rockie let the door fall shut behind her. "Two cracked ribs and a bruised diaphragm never killed anybody."

"Don't bet on it." Sheridan slid a hand beneath the thin sheet and blanket and rubbed his torso.

His chest was a mess of cuts, scrapes and blooming bruises. It was also broad, well muscled and lushly covered with dark hair.

"I brought you something." Rockie moved to the side of the bed and handed him a plastic sack. "Go ahead," she said when he eyed it dubiously. "It isn't ticking."

"Very funny." Sheridan opened the bag and took out a Chicago Cubs baseball cap. Regulation royal blue wool just like the pros wore, just like the one he'd lost.

He didn't know what to say. He was used to Wexlers who took, not gave. He ran his fingers back and forth across the bill and looked at Rockie.

Why wasn't he surprised that she dressed like a biker? Her black leather jacket had more buckles, chains and zippers than a dozen Hell's Angels; the skirt that matched it was snug and mini. The bruise showing around the edge of the Band-Aid stuck to the underside of her chin was the same shade of saffron yellow as her raw silk tank.

"You're welcome," she snapped abruptly, and wheeled toward the door.

She had amazingly long legs for such a little thing. Sleek and shapely in off-black stockings, cuffed socks that matched her tank top and—

"What the hell—" Sheridan winced and pushed himself up on his pillows to get a better look "—have you got on your feet?"

The patchwork leather tote bag on her shoulder bumped against her hip as she turned around, lifting an eyebrow and one spit-polished black foot. "Combat boots."

Sheridan hadn't seen a pair since he and the United States Navy had honorably and amicably parted company. He'd sure as hell never thought they were cute. Or sexy.

"Is that a fashion statement or did you enlist after breakfast?"

"Max took me shopping after breakfast. He bought them. He bought me this outfit, a couple others, and—"

The Cubs hat. She didn't say it, but her fingers caught in midpluck on the lapel of her jacket as she wheeled toward the door again.

"Hold it." Sheridan put the cap on as she turned around. "Thanks. It was nice of you to think of me."

Nice wasn't the word—disturbing was the word. Rockie wasn't about to tell Sheridan she'd thought about him and her father all night long as she'd lain awake too tired and strung out to sleep, afraid to close her eyes for fear she'd see Conan's smile. She never wanted to see it again. Not ever, not even in her nightmares.

She didn't want to feel her pulse skip as she looked at Sheridan, either, but it did. He was clean, shaved and one hell of a handsome pain in the ass. She hadn't noticed that yesterday under all the dirt and sweat. Well, once or twice. His thick dark hair was long and curled slightly around his ears and the back of his neck. In the sun it shone with red highlights.

He had a straight nose, a chiseled jaw and a wary set to his chin as he gazed at her intently, like he didn't quite know what to make of her. Rockie could relate to that. She didn't know what to make of him, either.

"You're welcome," she said again.

This time without the screw-you snap in her voice. She was plucking at her hair now, moussed to the max and finger-combed into stiff spikes over her forehead and around her ears. Sheridan didn't know much about her, except that she was Addison Wexler's daughter, that for some reason she thought it was cool to make herself up like Liza Minnelli and dress like Arnold Schwarzenegger in drag, and that her hair curled like a corkscrew when it got wet.

The bitch of it was he wanted to know more. Like what it felt like to kiss her mouth instead of her teeth. A sure sign that he was out of his ever-lovin' mind.

"We made headlines." She drew a newspaper out of her tote and walked to the bed. "Well, the quake did, anyway."

She handed him the paper, sat down in the high-backed, lime green convalescent chair by his bed, swung her tote on the floor and crossed her right knee over her left. Her skirt wasn't the miniest he'd ever seen by a long shot, but it hugged her like a banana skin.

Sheridan raised his left knee beneath the bedclothes and spread the paper against it. The headline read, Six Point Quake Rattles The Mojave, but that's all he could read without his half-lens professor glasses, the ugliest pair of horn-rims on the planet, which he'd bought to make himself look as old as possible in the classroom.

"Oops, almost forgot." She picked up her tote, rummaged inside for a brown leather eyeglass case, got up and handed it to him. "Max found your gear in the rented dune buggy."

"Thanks," he said. You, too, Max, he thought sourly, as he put them on and waited for her to burst out laughing.

"You're farsighted, aren't you?"

"Very." Sheridan glanced up at her from the newspaper. She wasn't laughing, not even smiling, just looking at him with her head cocked to one side. "How'd you know?"

"You weren't using binoculars up on the hill yesterday."

She wasn't as sharp as her old man, Sheridan decided, she was sharper. He had a feeling that might come in handy.

"There's nothing about the wrecked Apaches," she said as he scanned the article, "and no mention of a body found in the lab."

"It says here," Sheridan replied, quoting from the piece, "that 'employees report Dr. Addison Wexler left yesterday for an extended period of fieldwork.' It'll take a few days for the cops to get suspicious and dig deeper."

"I meant Conan," Rockie said quietly.

Sheridan laid the paper aside. Her eyes had that glassy, too-big-for-her-face look again.

"They may never find enough to sweep up and call human."

"Do you think he's dead?"

"I don't see how he could be alive."

Rockie couldn't, either. Still, she had a feeling, a very bad feeling, that sent a cold chill racing through her. She ducked her head and looked at her hands, clamped like claws around her knee. Her knuckles were white. She relaxed her fingers and watched the color come back.

So did Sheridan, wondering at the shiver that rippled her shoulders. "Where's Max?" he asked.

"Checking you out of here. He says we need to blow Barstow before the cops start asking questions. I'm not me, by the way. Max thought it was a good idea to hide Rockie Wexler in case Smith has some guys hanging around looking to grab me. I'm your fiancée Susie Wakefield. Your name is Phil Bevarly and Max is your brother Don. You and I got busted up four-wheeling in the desert during the quake."

"'Wake Up Little Susie,'" Sheridan said with a smile. "By the Everly Brothers, Don and Phil. Number one on the billboard charts in September, 1957."

"So you're the rock and roll fan," she said. "I thought it was Max."

"He likes jazz fusion."

"Yech." Rockie made a face as Maxwell came into the room with a pretty and plump blond nurse and Sheridan's gray nylon gym bag.

"'Morning, Phil," he said, swinging it onto the foot of the bed. "How's the ribs?"

"They hurt like hell, Don."

"I'll help you get dressed." The nurse glanced at Rockie. "Unless you'd like to, miss?"

"No." She shot out of the chair. "I mean, we're—uh—saving ourselves for our wedding night."

"How sweet," the nurse said.

I wouldn't, said the look the nurse gave Sheridan as she unzipped the gym bag. He smiled at her. Rockie grabbed her tote and left the room with Maxwell.

"I'll be outside smoking a cigarette," she said, reaching for the elevator call button.

Maxwell slapped his hand over it. "Not alone."

"Oh—yeah, right. I forgot," Rockie replied with a sheepish smile.

Maxwell gave her a that's-okay-you-little-nitwit pat on the arm and moved off to read the latest medical updates pinned to a nearby bulletin board. Rockie fished the fresh pack of cigarettes he'd bought her that morning out of her tote, held it under her nose and inhaled, deeply, until she was light-headed from the menthol in the filters.

Better than being light-headed at the thought of touching a man who didn't like her, a man who believed the sins of the father were visited on the child. She almost wished now that she didn't know what the chip was on Sheridan's shoulder.

She was beginning to get a bad feeling about her father's involvement with Smith, too. Not quite as bad as her feeling about Conan, but almost as scary. She still believed her father had had no idea what Smith planned to do with the TAQ box until it was too late. She didn't, either, not yet, but she was pretty sure it went way past wiping Wexler Technologies off the face of the earth.

Beyond that, Rockie didn't know what she believed—or who. She knew it sounded paranoid and ungrateful, but she couldn't help it. She'd discovered the connection between her father and Sheridan, but had no idea where Maxwell fit in, though she had a hunch he was more than Sheridan's sometimes employer.

She put her cigarettes back in her tote, glanced up and caught Maxwell staring at her. He didn't look away, not even when she walked up to him and asked, "Did my father steal the TAQ box from Sheridan?"

He didn't answer right away, just kept gazing at her. Rockie wished he'd at least blink. She was getting used to it, but the vacancy in his eyes was sometimes chilling.

"I think," he said finally, "that you should ask Sherry. Or your father."

"I figured if Conan knew, you would, too."

"Conan." There was almost a flicker in Maxwell's expressionless eyes. "But was he telling you the truth?"

"Based on Sheridan's reaction, I'd say yes."

"Then why are you asking me?" Maxwell gave her a smile as flat as his eyes and turned back to the bulletin board.

Because I don't trust you or Sheridan. I'm not even sure I trust my father, Rockie could have said, but didn't. There was no point, since Maxwell's answer made it pretty clear he already knew that.

So if she didn't trust them, why was she here? Why wasn't she looking for a pay phone to call the cops? Rockie had no idea, just a headache from lack of sleep, a bad case of confusion and frazzled nerves.

She was ready to scream for a cigarette by the time Sheridan appeared in his new Cubs hat, nicely worn jeans and a short-sleeve plaid shirt. Rockie felt a flush start up her neck when he caught her left hand in his right and laced them together. Just her guilty conscience, she told herself. The faint tremor in his fingers she wrote off to weakness, or maybe a desire to choke her.

He was only playing a part, making it look good for the nurse watching them from the desk as they moved toward the elevator. And for Maxwell, too, but he was no more fooled than Rockie. When the elevator came, he stepped into it and glanced at Sheridan over his shoulder.

"I'll bring the car up front. Take your time. Maybe a wheelchair, too."

"Take a hike, Mother Maxwell," Sheridan growled at him as the elevator doors slid shut and he pushed the button to go down.

"Oh, Mr. Bevarly. Miss Wakefield." The plump blonde pressed the Hold button on the phone and stepped toward them around her desk. "Have you a few minutes?"

"Is there a problem?" Sheridan gave Rockie's fingers a let-me-do-the-talking squeeze.

"Oh, no," she replied with a smile. "There's a Detective Sergeant Cummings on the line. He'd like to talk to you about the earthquake and a backpack they found out in the desert near the quake site. He said he can be here in about five minutes. He'd like to speak to you if—"

"Tell him fine, we'll wait," Sheridan said, cutting her off as the elevator doors opened. "My brother Don went for the car. We'll tell him and be right back."

He hustled Rockie into the empty car, pushed Lobby and said "Shit" between his teeth as the doors closed.

"We aren't going to wait, are we?" Rockie asked.

"Hell, no. We're gettin' outta Dodge in the Dodge."

"Won't we look guilty if we don't talk to him?"

"We're already guilty. As phony IDs go, Don and Phil Bevarly are pretty solid. Max and I have used them before, but there's only our word that you're Susie Wakefield. When that breaks down, so will Don and Phil. The hospital could make a neat little case for falsifying medical records."

"But we had a good reason."

Boy, did that sound stupid. Rockie couldn't believe she'd said it. The look Sheridan gave her said he couldn't, either.

"That won't mean shit to the cops. If they found your backpack, they've probably found the Apaches, too. And eight dead men. They'll want to know why we didn't report that."

"Oh. Yeah, I guess they will."

Rockie ducked her chin to hide the pang of guilt that brought tears to her eyes. She was alive, but the troopers who'd stood grinning at her yesterday as she'd climbed up on the boulder weren't. She hadn't known any of them, and their deaths weren't her fault; still, she felt sick with remorse that she'd forgotten all about them.

"Your gun was in the backpack. Is it licensed?"

Rockie nodded, blinking to clear her eyes.

"Then if they haven't already, it won't take the cops long to run the serial number and find out it's registered to Addison Wexler's daughter. He's vanished, his lab is a pile of rubble, eight guys are dead and you were in the thick of it with a gun. Any questions?"

"Only one." Rockie raised just her eyes to look at Sheridan. "When your ribs are healed can I hit you as hard as I can in the gut?"

"You can hit me now." He tapped his chin with an index finger as the elevator stopped and the doors opened. "Right here."

"I'll wait." Rockie swept ahead of him out of the car. "I want to make sure I hit you where it's going to hurt the most."

"Believe me, kid," Sheridan said wearily behind her. "You already have."

10

MAXWELL HAD WARNED HER. Still, the shock of seeing her apartment ransacked hit Rockie like a fist. She stood in the doorway staring at the shambles, clenching and unclenching her hands, fighting the urge to scream and belt Maxwell.

"If I were Conan, I would've snatched you for insurance at the same time I grabbed Addison," he'd told her in the rental car on their way from LAX. "The only thing that saved you was leaving for your father's lab when you did. I'm sure Conan's boys weren't happy to find you gone. I'm also sure they left you a calling card. It won't be easy, but if it's there, we need to see it."

This was twice in twenty-four hours Smith had trashed her life. It was, Rockie swore, the last time.

"Just this once," Maxwell said behind her, "I wish I'd been wrong."

"Just this once," she replied, "so do I."

Sheridan heard the flat edge in her voice and figured it for either shock or outrage. He'd already checked the bathroom and bedroom, finished his sweep of the kitchen and stepped over a pile of broken blue stoneware into the living room. He saw Rockie standing in the open doorway with Max. Her hands were white knuckled fists, her eyes huge.

"It's clean," he said. "No bugs or booby traps."

That surprised him. After yesterday, he'd expected at least one welcome-home present from Conan. He watched Rockie step into the mess, her gaze skittering over slashed furniture, overturned tables, broken lamps and shredded books. She clenched her jaw and stuffed her hands in her jacket pockets.

Sheridan moved to the bar that separated the living room from the kitchen, picked up the receiver of the white Art Deco phone next to the answering machine and listened to the dial tone. "Still connected. Funny they missed this."

"Maybe they didn't," Maxwell replied, then asked Rockie, "Where do I find the manager?"

"Mrs. Riley's in 1-D, around back."

"I doubt she heard anything, but I'll ask. Gather up anything you want in one suitcase." He took the car keys out of his pocket and gave them to her. "Put your bag in the trunk. I'll meet you at the car."

"Where are we going?" Rockie asked, looking at him over her shoulder.

"I'll tell you later." Maxwell half turned in the doorway, gave Sheridan a stay-with-her nod and left.

Rockie put the keys in her pocket and hugged her biker jacket closer. "Why's he so cryptic all of a sudden?"

"It isn't all of a sudden." Sheridan hung up the phone and stepped away from the bar. "He's always cryptic."

"Do you know where we're going?"

"Haven't a clue."

Her gaze moved around the room again, this time more slowly. "What d'you suppose they were looking for?"

He considered lying to her, but changed his mind. Time to see how much she could take, where her breaking point was.

"Nothing. This isn't a while-we're-here-let's-see-what-we-can-find kind of job. This is a let's scare the hell out of her and show her who she's dealing with job."

"Have you ever done anything like this?"

He had, once. When he'd read about Addison Wexler's Nobel prize and realized his long-festering suspicions weren't just suspicions. He'd laid the newspaper aside and trashed his whole house.

"No," he lied.

She turned her head slightly to one side and slid her right eyebrow up a fraction. She didn't believe him. He didn't blame her.

"So this is supposed to scare me into what? Running out of here right into Smith's hands?"

"Probably."

"It won't work."

We'll see, Sheridan thought. He knew she had guts. He also knew she leapt before she looked and did stupid things like crawl out on a boulder just to call his bluff.

Because he had a similar streak in his nature, Sheridan recognized her tendency toward impulse. And the danger in it. Being Wexler's kid, he'd figured she was smart. While the ER doctor had sewn up her chin, Max had told him just how smart. She hid it well, he thought, watching her drop to her heels and scoop up a pile of slashed typewritten sheets.

"What's that? Your memoirs?"

"Hardly." She tossed him a smirk and slid the pages into a ripped and gouged green binder. "It's a script. I'm—I mean I *was*—an actress."

"Oh, yeah? So what are you now?"

"A homeless person for starters." Rockie tried but couldn't quite manage a smile around the tremble in her chin. "Maybe an orphan, too."

"Addison is all Smith has at the moment. So long as the disks stay out of his clutches, Addison stays alive."

"Are you sure about that?"

"'Bout eighty-three percent."

"I wish you wouldn't be so damn precise," she snapped irritably.

"Fine." Sheridan shrugged. "I'll lie to you."

"No. Don't lie to me." Rockie clutched the script and shot to her feet. "I'm sick of people lying to me."

Sheridan didn't say anything, just looked at her, a curious arch in one eyebrow. Rockie spun away from him, hugging the script to keep her fingers from shaking.

She couldn't get Maxwell's question out of her mind, even though she knew damn good and well why she couldn't just turn around and ask Sheridan about the TAQ box. She wasn't ready yet to face the possibility that her father was a thief. Maybe she could once Addison Wexler was safe, but not now.

"This ought to pass for a burglary," Sheridan said. "The cops should buy it, so your insurance company—"

"No cops." Rockie laid the script aside and crammed her hands back in her pockets. "Maybe later, when this is over."

She still couldn't face Sheridan, or the thought of insurance adjusters and claim forms. She had no idea how in hell she was going to replace her Jeep, her furniture, all her clothes and other belongings without a settlement, but that was the least of her worries.

"Could I be alone for a few minutes?"

Sheridan didn't answer. Rockie waited, sensing his hesitation. He doesn't trust me, she thought, any more than I trust him. He'd made it clear yesterday he didn't want to help her, although he had. She couldn't figure out why he'd come or why he was still here.

"I'm not going to steal the silver." Rockie shot him a look over her shoulder. "It's all bent and twisted in a pile on the floor. Besides, it's *my* silver. I bought and paid for it. Want to see the receipt?"

Sheridan's jasper eyes narrowed, a muscle jumped in his jaw. Just once, then he had it under control.

"Don't get snippy with me, kid. I'm not the one who trashed your place."

"And I'm not the one who stole the TAQ box from you."

"I never said Addison stole anything from anybody."

"You didn't have to. The look on your face when Conan told me said it for you." Rockie turned toward him, her hands like ice in her pockets. She hadn't meant to start this, but she might as well finish it. "I knew I'd heard your name, but it took me a while to remember that one of Dad's assistants met you at a seminar. She said *you* said you gave up on the TAQ box when it proved risky and unreliable. Did you?"

"What difference does it make?" Sheridan's jaw twitched again. "It's ancient history."

"I don't think so. You've been at my throat from the start, and I want to know why. Is it me, or is it my father?"

"Maybe it's a little bit of both."

His answer didn't surprise Rockie, but it stung. She'd felt the same way once before, when she'd almost bumped into Robert Redford in the supermarket and he'd looked at her like she was a loaf of day-old bread.

"Well, that's a relief. I thought maybe you were bent out of shape because my father picked up and perfected something you'd discarded."

Sheridan's jaw stopped twitching and clenched like a vice. Bull's-eye, Rockie thought. In the ego or the temper. Or maybe both, she decided, watching warning red flecks flash in his eyes.

"Take all the time you want," he said, striding past her toward the door. "I'll go talk to the landlady with Max."

"Just tell me one thing." Rockie wheeled after him. "You don't like me, you don't like my father, you've made it abundantly clear that you don't want anything to do with either one of us, so what the hell are you doing here?"

Sheridan opened the door, looked back at her and smiled. "Enjoying every second of this."

Rockie expected him to slam the door. Instead, he shut it behind him with a quiet click.

The stitches in her chin hurt, so bad her throat ached. At least she told herself that's what the pain was, then she picked her way across the littered carpet, knelt next to a hewn-in-two table and picked up a handful of broken porcelain that used to be a trinket box shaped like a butterfly.

Her mother had kept it on her dressing table. Rockie had found one of her baby teeth in it. She'd thrown the tooth away, but she'd kept the box. Now all she had was a handful of shards. She closed her fingers around them and blinked back tears. No matter how this ended up, Rockie had a sinking feeling things would never be the same again.

The last decision she'd made was to leave L.A. for Barstow. Everything that had happened since had been dictated by circumstance or someone else. None of it had been her fault—or her choice—yet the course of her life had irrevocably changed.

The phone rang, startling Rockie to her feet. In the movies the bad guys always ripped the phone out of the wall. Sheridan said it was funny it was still connected, but Rockie didn't think so. She thought it was deliberate, and almost fell over a broken cane-backed bar stool hurrying to answer it on the second ring. "Hello?"

"Good afternoon, Rockie. My name is Greer Hanlon. We've never met, but—"

"I know who you are. I saw you at the lab once." A picture of Smith's fair-haired, perfectly pin-striped assistant stretching out of the limo flashed through Rockie's head. "Where's my father?"

"Here with me. If time allows, I'll let you speak to him. Gregarious as Mrs. Riley is, I doubt she'll be able to detain Maxwell and Dr. Sheridan long."

Holy shit, Rockie thought, her heart dropping to her toes, Smith's goons are watching the building. Like its neighbors, this one had open stairwells and landings. Only a driveway and a low wall on the south and another low wall overhung by bougainvillea on the north separated them.

"What do you want?" Rockie asked, wetting her suddenly dry lips.

"The disks, of course."

"I don't have them." Her gaze shot to her tote bag on the floor by the door where she'd dropped it. The disks were in it, in a plastic case Maxwell had given her to protect them. "They're with Conan at the bottom of the crater that used to be my father's lab."

"Conan? Oh. You mean my chief of security. He'd be flattered." Hanlon chuckled. "Nice try, but he didn't have the disks when we found him. I want them."

"I want my father, you son of a bitch."

"I want to give him to you, Miss Wexler, and I will, in exchange for the disks."

"I told you I don't have them."

"Get them. Bring them to the Griffith Park Observatory in half an hour. I'll meet you on the terraces."

"Wait a minute." Rockie uncurled the twenty-foot cord from the base of the phone and stepped to the living room window.

She couldn't see anyone watching the building, just a man in the backyard next door watering the grass, and the copper dome of the Observatory through a haze of smog, high on the tree-crested Hollywood Hills.

"I want to talk to my father first."

"There isn't time. You have only half an hour to get your hands on the disks. You'll see him soon."

"I'm not going anywhere until I talk to him."

"He's perfectly fine, and he'll stay that way so long as you do exactly as I say. Come alone, by the way, or you'll never see him again. Not alive."

"Listen, you—"

The line went dead.

"Shit!" Rockie wheeled back to the bar and slammed the phone on its cradle.

She stood clutching the receiver, her heart banging, seconds ticking off inside her head. She was beginning to feel like a time bomb. A terrified, who-do-I-trust, which-end-is-up time bomb.

The probability that Hanlon was lying about exchanging her father for the disks was higher than Rockie liked to think about, so she didn't. Instead she sprinted across the room, swung her tote off the floor with one hand and opened the door with the other. She started through it, then whirled abruptly back and bolted for the bathroom.

She wished she had time to throw up. She knew Hanlon would say or do anything to get his hands on her and/or the disks, but there was a chance—albeit a slim one—that he was willing to deal. She'd trust that chance and do exactly what he said—to a point.

The bathroom was a disaster, the towels and shower curtain slashed and reeking of mouthwash and bubble bath. Rockie slipped in a puddle, caught herself on the sink as she went down on her knees and groped in the vanity underneath for the box of tampons she kept in a back corner.

It was still there, untouched. So was the wad of emergency cash she kept rubber banded around her duplicate American Express card. Sometimes it paid to be paranoid.

Next she rooted through the broken and emptied cosmetic bottles strewn everywhere until she found a purse-size can of hair spray. She shook it close to her ear, prayed it had enough propellant left to be useful, shoved it in her tote along with the money, raced for the stairs, and downed them so fast she nearly collided with a terra-cotta planter overflowing with white petunias at the bottom.

Catching the corner of the building to stop herself, Rockie peeked around it to make sure the coast was clear. She didn't see Sheridan or Maxwell, just two LAPD uniform cops walking briskly up the driveway toward the building. She didn't recognize the one on the right, but she did the one on the left.

It was the blond crew-cut trooper with the Robert DeNiro mole.

11

PANIC MADE ROCKIE'S heart clutch—self-preservation sent her whirling down the half flight of steps behind her into the narrow walkway that led to the storage lockers. She flattened herself against the shadowed wall just as the cops drew even with the stairwell entrance. The one she didn't recognize kept on walking toward the rear of the building and Mrs. Riley's apartment, the blond trooper turned up the steps.

Rockie leaned far enough out of her hiding place to watch him climb toward her apartment on the third floor. When he stepped out of her sight, she bolted up the steps and shot a look around the corner of the building. The second cop had disappeared around back—a black-and-white squad car sat parked at the curb behind the blue Chevy Caprice Maxwell had rented at LAX.

When she heard the blond trooper knock on her door, Rockie sprinted for the curb, fishing the keys out of her pocket, feeling eyes on her back. The car was unlocked. A stupid thing to do in L.A., but she was grateful. She opened the door, threw her tote inside, slid behind the wheel, started the engine, shoved the gear-shift into Drive and trod on the gas.

She left three feet of rubber, the phony cops, Sheridan, Maxwell and the shreds of her life behind her. "Good luck, fellas," Rockie murmured as she braked at the stop sign at the end of the block and made a squealing turn toward Griffith Park.

Keeping her left hand on the wheel, she rooted the disks out of her tote with her right and tucked them in the inside pocket of her jacket. One-handed, Rockie lit a cigarette and tucked her butane lighter in her left pocket. The can of hair spray and her pack of cigarettes she slipped into her right, and she gave that pocket a reassuring pat. Smith wasn't the only one who believed in insurance.

Since it was Wednesday afternoon, traffic on the canyon roads was light. Twenty-two minutes had ticked off the dashboard clock when Rockie wheeled the Chevy into the Griffith Park Observatory lot. She found a space near the front, bailed out of the car, dropped the keys in her outside breast pocket, left the doors unlocked and ran for the copper-domed building.

From the terraces built along the back, the view of the Los Angeles basin stretching to the horizon was staggering. So was Rockie by the time she came to a winded, flat-footed stop. There were a few tourists milling around admiring the view. None of them was Addison Wexler.

She wasn't surprised, just bitterly disappointed. Tears sprang in her eyes, but she blinked them away as Greer Hanlon turned from the balustrade and came toward her. No pinstripes today, just olive trousers, a yellow polo shirt and loafers with no socks.

A mountain of steroids with legs and spiked platinum hair followed. His jeans and Gold's Gym T-shirt were heat creased, his white Nikes scuffed. If Conan was safely buried in a grave, Rockie thought, he'd be rolling over in it.

"Hello, Rockie." Hanlon stopped in front of her, Mount Anabolic beside him. "Do you have the disks?"

"Right here." She opened her jacket and lifted the plastic case high enough to show him. "Where's my father?"

"Rockie." Hanlon looked at her askance. "Surely you realize I couldn't trust you to come alone."

"Why not? I trusted you."

"You had no choice. Your father's waiting for you just a few blocks from here. I'll take you to him."

"No way." Rockie shrugged off the hand he lifted to take her elbow. "We'll do the trade right here, on the terrace, like you said, or the disks and I are outta here."

"The information on them must be verified and authenticated. I'm not about to do that out here."

"My father's life is on the line, Hanlon. Why in hell would I try to pass off bogus disks?"

"I don't know." He tilted his head and eyed her curiously. "Why did your father try it?"

If Smith didn't beat her to it, Rockie swore she'd kill Addison Wexler. With her bare hands. Just as soon as she saved her father's neck, she'd wring it. Cheerfully.

"These are the disks I took out of his office. I swear they haven't been tampered with or altered."

"I'd like to believe you, Rockie. Really I would. But I'm not taking a Wexler's word for anything."

"Well, I like *this*," she shot back indignantly. "A kidnapper and a killer calling *me* a liar."

"I haven't killed anyone."

"Oh, really? How about Conan and the eight mercenaries in those two Apaches?"

"They were well paid to take risks. Gino," Hanlon said, and the mountain loomed toward her.

"Hold it." Rockie skittered out of reach. "Gimme a minute to think."

"Gino," Hanlon said again. The mountain stopped and stepped back beside him.

Right where Rockie wanted him. The slim chance she'd trusted—if it had ever existed—had vanished. Time to trust Sheridan's eighty-three percent surety that so long as the disks stayed out of Smith's hands her father would stay alive—and pray that Sheridan wouldn't kill her for ditching him and Maxwell. Rockie was a hundred percent certain he'd want to, but only fifty percent sure he wouldn't.

"Can I smoke?" she asked.

"Show me the pack."

Rockie took it out of her pocket and handed it to him. Hanlon opened it, then gave it back.

"Gino," he said, and the mountain took a lighter out of his pocket and spun the wheel.

Rockie shook out a cigarette and leaned the tip into the flame. Gino reeked of English Leather and suntan oil. Sucking smoke into her mouth, she stepped back, her heart pounding.

"Once you've made sure the disks are real, then what?"

"Then you and your father are free to go."

"I'd like to believe you, Greer. Really I would," Rockie said, tossing his words back at him. "But I'm not taking a Hanlon's word for anything."

"Touché." He smiled, his brown eyes crinkling with amusement. "How about the word of Winston Kimball?"

"Is that Winston Kimball, aka Mr. Smith?"

Hanlon nodded. Rockie's throat went dry. That clinches it, she thought, willing her fingers not to shake as she drew on her cigarette. If Hanlon intended to let her go, no way would he tell her Smith's real name. Winston Kimball meant nothing to her, though the tone of Hanlon's voice suggested she ought to fall on her knees.

"How about restitution for my totaled Jeep and trashed apartment?"

Hanlon laughed. Rockie slipped the cigarette pack in her right-hand pocket and closed her fingers around the hair-spray can. Pinching her cigarette between the first two fingers of her left hand, she smiled and hooked her thumb in her pocket.

"Just like your father," Hanlon said, shaking his head. "I suppose you have a figure in mind?"

"Of course." Rockie parked her cigarette in the corner of her mouth and let her left hand slip oh so casually into her pocket. "Twenty thousand should do it."

"Sounds fair. Twenty thousand it is. Shall we?" He lifted his hand but made no move to touch her, just gestured toward the east end of the terrace.

"Sure thing."

It would be, Rockie thought, if she timed it right. When she took a step toward them, Hanlon and Gino turned and separated to give her room to walk between them. When she took another, so did they. When they took a third, she stopped and whipped out the hair spray and her lighter. Hanlon glanced back at her—she flicked the lighter and pressed the button on the can.

A tongue of flame shot toward his face. Hanlon screamed. So did a gray-haired woman in Bermuda shorts standing nearby taking pictures. When Gino spun toward her, Rockie threw the can at him. He brushed it away and lunged. Terrified, Rockie stabbed her cigarette into his left cheek.

He howled and she ran, her stomach heaving from the smell of burning hair and the after image of her cigarette stuck to Gino's face. Legs and arms pumping, the buckles and chains on her jacket bouncing and jangling, she flew back the way she'd come, around the west corner of the Observatory and straight into Sheridan's arms.

It was like running into a rock. A grim-faced, tight-lipped rock, with his ball cap turned backward on his head. Rockie barely had time to snatch a startled breath before he grabbed her and flung her against the building. Hard enough to slam the wind out of her.

She saw stars and Sheridan slide up against the wall beside her. His left arm was raised and bent at the elbow—until Gino came rocketing around the corner, then it flashed out in a perfect clothesline and caught him in the throat. His feet shot out from under him and he keeled over on his back, his skull making a sickening thud on the concrete.

"Gimme the car keys," Sheridan said, already running as he yanked her off the wall.

She fished them out of her pocket and dropped them in his hand. His grip on her tightened, and his stride lengthened as he half pulled, half pushed her up the walkway beside him and across the parking lot. When they reached the blue Chevy, he opened the driver's door, shoved her inside, jumped in after her, stuck the key in the ignition, started the engine, threw the transmission into Reverse and smoked the tires backing out of the space.

All in less time than it took Rockie to struggle herself out of the heap he'd pushed her into on the bench seat and suck the first deep breath she'd managed since she'd raced across the terrace. She felt faint, wanted to stick her head between her knees, but didn't. Instead, she scrambled around and looked at Sheridan, his jasper eyes fixed on the rearview mirror as he adjusted it and screeched the Chevy through the first curve in the canyon road.

"Before you kill me," Rockie said, gasping for air, "I have a name for you. Winston Kimball."

"Winston Kimball?" Sheridan repeated it warily. "Are you *sure?* Who told you?"

"Greer Hanlon, Smith—I mean, Kimball's—assistant." Rockie swallowed hard. "The guy whose eyebrows I melted."

"That was a nice piece of work."

"It was not *nice*. It worked. Period."

Sheridan squealed the Chevy through another curve and glanced at her. His eyes were mostly green. Rockie swallowed again, shivering despite the sweat gluing her silk tank to her breastbone, and turned her head to look out the side window.

Nice work, indeed. The Rockie Wexler who'd improvised a blowtorch and used it on another human being wasn't what she wanted to be. She preferred the old model, the one who hadn't been able to shoot Conan, even when her life had depended on it. The new one scared the hell out of her.

"Hanlon's damn lucky he got you instead of Max," Sheridan said. "He'd be missing more than eyebrows."

A mental picture of Maxwell's lifeless cobalt eyes made Rockie shiver again. "Where is he?"

"Mopping up Mrs. Riley's driveway with the two phony cops Hanlon sent to take care of the Bevarly Brothers."

"I recognized the blond trooper from the gate at the lab. If I hadn't looked around the corner of the building first . . ."

Rockie let the thought trail off. Just yesterday, she'd yearned for badges and uniforms. So much for things you know you can trust, she thought bitterly.

"Wonder where they got the cop car?" she asked.

"Stole it probably," Sheridan replied, glancing down at the speedometer which hovered near fifty.

Her heart and her pulse had stopped pounding, the muscles in her calves were no longer shuddering. The throb in her back from her rough collision with the Observatory wall had eased to a dull ache, and she could breathe without thinking about it. A damn good thing, since her brain felt just as blurred as the tree-lined curb streaming past the car—until she heard the wail of a siren.

Panic sent her heart and her pulse leaping again, until she realized the siren was ahead of them, not behind them. She sighed audibly with relief as the Chevy slid through another curve and she saw a black-and-white squad car coming at them, lights flashing, siren screaming. As it shot past, the officer behind the wheel, wearing a uniform with a sergeant's chevron on the sleeve, lifted a hand to them.

It was Maxwell.

12

THE SHOCK OF SEEING him behind the wheel cleared Rockie's head like a glass of ice water thrown in her face. Her mind flashed back to Sheridan's comment about the phone. She'd seen him lift the receiver and listen, but she'd turned away then to take the car keys from Maxwell. Sheridan must have bugged the phone while her back was turned.

"You son of a bitch," Rockie breathed shakily, her fists clenching in her lap. "You son of a *bitch!*"

Flinging herself sideways on the seat, she threw a punch at Sheridan's face. It would've landed squarely on his jaw if he hadn't caught it in his right hand. The nose of the blue Chevy swerved toward the double yellow line, but he hauled it back and glared at her.

"Calm down before you get us killed."

"Isn't that what you set me up for?" Rockie tried but couldn't wrench her fist out of Sheridan's grip.

There was no trace of the tremble she'd idiotically wished was attraction when he'd taken her hand in the hospital in Barstow. His fingers were clamped around hers like talons.

"You were never in danger," he said. "I was right behind you the whole time."

"The hell you were!" Rockie gave up on her right and slugged him with her left. The blow landed on his arm, hard enough to pop her knuckles, but Sheridan only glowered.

"Next time you steal a car, look in the trunk first. You never know who might be in it."

Rockie stopped struggling and blinked at him, taken aback but still angry. "I hope I hit every pothole in the road."

"Don't worry. You did." Sheridan's mouth twisted sourly and he let go of her hand.

Rockie yanked it away from him, grabbed the armrest on the passenger door and pulled herself away from him. "You knew Hanlon would call, didn't you? You and Maxwell. You set me up," she repeated.

"We guessed he'd take one last shot at you and the disks. The phone merely clinched it. We didn't set you up. We just made it easy for you."

"How did you know I'd agree to meet him?"

Rockie wasn't sure what she expected Sheridan to say, but his quiet "Under the circumstances, anybody would" surprised her and brought tears to her eyes.

"Why didn't you tell me? If I'd known I—"

Rockie caught herself and bit her lip. She couldn't say she wouldn't have set fire to Greer Hanlon's hair because she wasn't at all sure that if she found herself in the same predicament she wouldn't do it again. In a heartbeat.

"The less you knew the better," Sheridan replied. "The less you'd be able to tell Hanlon if things went wrong."

"How big was the if?"

"Fifty-fifty."

Slowly, very slowly, this was beginning to make sense. Rockie was still angry, still felt betrayed, but she was willing to hear him out before she slugged him again.

"Why did you make it easy for me?"

"It was the best way to find out what Smith has in his arsenal since he lost Conan and his mercs, and how serious a threat he thinks Max and I are."

They were nearly halfway down the canyon, the Chevy still rocketing along near fifty. Sheridan took a last look in his mirror and eased on the brake.

"So what's the verdict?" Rockie asked.

"Hard to say." One-handed, Sheridan swept off his Cubs hat, raked his hair back, turned the cap around and put it back on. "Either Smith's intelligence isn't that good or he's arrogant as hell. If he is Winston Kimball, then my money's on arrogant. He only sent three guys after me and Max. The two cops and the guy watering the grass next door. There was no tail on you. Gino was Hanlon's only backup."

"What's Max doing at the Observatory?"

"Damage control. Everybody trusts cops, except maybe Hanlon and Gino." Sheridan smiled wistfully. "I'd love to see their faces when Sergeant Maxwell shows up."

"He isn't—I mean, he won't—I mean . . ."

"He won't," Sheridan finished for her. "You don't kill the messenger. At least not until he delivers the message."

And after that, Rockie wondered, but didn't ask. Instead, she asked, "What message?"

"Simply this." Sheridan braked at the stop sign at the bottom of the canyon and checked the traffic before making a left toward the freeway and LAX. "The next time Hanlon or Smith—or Winston Kimball, or whoever the hell he is—comes after you and the disks, he better come with a battalion of marines."

Delivered by Sheridan, with red flecks flashing in his narrowed jasper gaze, the message gave Rockie chills. Delivered by Maxwell with his dead-inside cobalt eyes, it gave a whole new meaning to the word threat.

"Do you think Kimball has one?" she asked. "A battalion, I mean."

"We'll find out."

There was enough of an ominous undertone in Sheridan's voice to send a flood of gooseflesh shooting through Rockie. And a sudden, half-sick feeling.

"Where does this leave my father?"

"At this point, that's up to Addison. If I were him, I'd pretend I'd suddenly come to my senses, play along and pray to God Max can find me and get me out. Whether he will or not is anybody's guess. Addison is as used to making rules and calling shots as Winston Kimball."

The name still meant nothing to Rockie, although she had a feeling it should. "Who is Winston Kimball, anyway?"

"A billionaire damn-the-environment-full-speed-ahead lunatic. Heavy into oil prospecting. Especially in North Africa. Particularly the Sahara."

"What does oil prospecting have to do with earthquakes and the TAQ box?"

"Haven't a clue, but I'm not a lunatic."

"Yeah, you're a pain in the ass."

Sheridan's chin shot toward her. So quickly, Rockie jumped, startled—and amazed. He wasn't frowning or glaring at her. He was smiling, the first genuine, honest-to-God smile she'd ever seen on his face.

"Damn straight. And don't forget it."

"Not likely."

Nor was it likely, once this was over, that she'd ever see Sheridan again. She'd known him scarcely twenty-four hours. Still, the thought of never seeing him glower at her again made Rockie's stomach clutch. It was nothing more than stress-induced dependency. Rockie knew that, but it didn't help.

"So how do we find out if Smith really is Kimball?"

"Hopefully, the disks will tell us something. It's time we found a computer and had a look at them."

Panic seized Rockie, until she clutched the front of her jacket and felt them, hard and safe in their plastic case, in her inside pocket.

"Don't worry." Sheridan glanced at her as she tugged her tote off the floor and zipped the disks into a side pocket. "Just in case, Max copied them last night while you were getting your chin sewn up."

It was the logical thing to do, yet it irked Rockie. She still didn't trust Maxwell or Sheridan completely, but knowing they didn't trust her was insulting and infuriating. Intellectually there was no good reason why they should trust her, but the fact that they didn't tied her emotions in knots. If she could just figure out what was in this for them, if she understood their motives, she felt sure she could resolve her twisted, jumbled feelings. Not to mention sprout wings and fly.

"Max has a nifty little IBM clone on his Lear jet." Sheridan rubbed his ribs with his right hand as he braked at a stoplight. "It's parked at LAX. He'll meet us there, and then we'll take a look at the disks."

"What did he do with the Raptor?" Rockie asked. "Fold it up and put it in his pocket?"

"Wouldn't surprise me." Sheridan winced and lifted his hand to the steering wheel. "I don't know where he keeps it hangared. Nobody does."

"I thought the attendants were going to cross themselves when he set it down on the chopper pad at the hospital. He came back pretty quick after he dropped us off, you know. Doesn't sound like he had far to go, does it?"

She glanced at Sheridan, saw him wincing and wiggling his little finger in his left ear. He wasn't paying any attention to her, or to the traffic in the left-turn lane, sweeping through the intersection with the arrow.

A good way to get rear ended in L.A. was to be slow coming off a stoplight. Rockie opened her mouth to tell him the light was about to change, but got distracted by a woman walking a black standard poodle along the sidewalk.

The dog was all over the place, leaping and jumping in circles, barking and twisting its leash around the woman's legs. She stopped, shaking a scolding finger and trying to untangle herself. The poodle paid no attention to her, just sat back on its haunches, lifted its head and howled. Mournfully. Again and again.

Rockie looked quickly from the dog to the stoplight suspended above the intersection. It was quivering and swaying from side to side, but there was no wind. The day was calm, warm and smoggy, but calm. The poodle kept howling.

"Uh-oh," she said, a shiver zipping up her spine, a quaver in her voice as the Chevy began to shimmy.

In the middle of the intersection, a manhole cover blew sky-high, a plume of sewer gas shooting after it.

The driver of the Ford Escort in front of them threw open his door and ran for the sidewalk.

"Bail out!" Rockie cried, shouldering her door open.

"Relax." Sheridan caught her elbow. "It's just a little tremor."

"Yeah, right," Rockie retorted, yanking free of him. "Just like the staircase in the lab is strong enough to hold us."

With several other drivers panicked by the tremor, she sprinted across two lanes of stopped traffic toward the sidewalk. By the time she reached it, the stoplight had stopped swinging, the manhole cover was rolling away down the street, and the poodle had stopped howling. The dog sprang up, shook himself and gave his mistress a tongue-lolling, don't-know-what-came-over-me look from under his curly, shaggy bang.

"Just a tremor," said one of the other motorists with a nervous laugh as he stepped off the curb and headed back to his car.

Rockie followed him, her heart still banging, her nerves still jumping. Born and raised in California, she'd never, *ever* freaked at the tremors that jiggled L.A. as often as traffic snarled on the freeways. After yesterday's quake, she supposed her panicked reaction was perfectly natural, but still she felt her cheeks flame as she slid back into the Chevy beside Sheridan.

"How'd you know?" she asked as she slammed the door and hooked her seat belt.

"I've got a knack for it." He shrugged as traffic began moving, and he eased the Chevy carefully around the open manhole. "I spend a lot of time studying quakes and tremors. I've developed an affinity."

So had her father. Every time a tremor rolled through the Mojave, Wexler and his assistants laid bets on how strong it was before clustering around the seismograph to watch it spit data. Her father always won.

"So that's what you do when you're not working for Maxwell, huh? You're a seismologist."

"No. I teach geology."

"So tell me, Dr. Sheridan. Was this tremor natural or manmade?"

"Dunno. Once I've had a look at the seismograph printouts from this one and yesterday's quake, I might."

"What d'you think they'll tell you?"

"Beats me. Only one thing's for sure at this point."

"What's that?" Rockie asked, not at all sure she wanted to know.

"Conan said as much." Sheridan flipped on the turn signal, made a right onto a freeway ramp and shot her a somber, sidelong look. "The best weapon in Smith's arsenal is the TAQ box."

13

IS THIS THE BIG ONE?

The Associated Press

GOLDEN, COLORADO—The earthquake measuring 6.2 on the Richter scale that rattled California's Mojave Desert on Tuesday and caused mild aftershocks in Los Angles on Wednesday has seismologists with the U.S. Geological Survey nervous. And more than a little puzzled.

"Earthquakes can occur anywhere at any time," said Dr. Fred Eddings of the USGS. "What's odd about the Mojave quake is that it occurred in an area with little previous seismic activity. We were not expecting a quake of this magnitude to occur here. It was a real surprise."

The USGS has dispatched field teams to investigate and monitor any further activity in the Mojave Desert. Theories as to the cause of the quake vary from a heretofore unknown and undocumented fault line to unusually strong sunspot activity.

"DON'T FORGET VOODOO, boys." Sheridan took off his glasses, stuck them on top of his head, rubbed his tired eyes and tossed the Friday morning edition of the Springfield, Missouri *News-Leader* headline-down on the hardwood floor of his study. With ease, he could read the companion story below the fold:

NOBEL LAUREATE AND DAUGHTER MISSING AFTER QUAKE

BARSTOW, CA—Authorities continue their search for Dr. Addison Wexler, 57, and his daughter, Rochelle, 26, both missing since Tuesday's earthquake destroyed the Wexler Technologies laboratory in the Mojave Desert.

Ironically, employees first reported Dr. Wexler had taken a sabbatical to field-test a device designed to predict quakes, but repeated appeals to him broadcast on television and radio have gone unanswered.

Also missing from her North Hollywood apartment is Wexler's daughter, Rochelle. It is believed that Miss Wexler may have joined her father for the field tests, which Wexler Technologies staff members say are always conducted in extremely remote and quake-prone areas.

Anyone with information regarding the whereabouts of Dr. Addison Wexler or his daughter, Rochelle, are asked to contact their nearest FBI regional office.

"Just ask for the spin doctor who wrote this article," Sheridan said disgustedly as he dropped his gaze to the side-by-side photographs of father and daughter printed below the article.

Wexler's photo was the one he'd seen in countless scientific journals and newsmagazines. It showed a handsome, distinguished man with a clipped mustache and salt-and-pepper hair. The one of Rockie he supposed had come from her college yearbook. It had that angled head and loftily lifted chin look of every magna cum laude photo he'd ever seen, his own included. Except he'd worn a Maltese cross pierced through his left lobe and tied his shoulder-length hair in a black ribbon at the nape of his neck.

Rockie's hair was just about the same length in her photo, a long, sleek style with the sides drawn up in barrettes and a fringe of bangs. He decided he liked her Liza Minnelli cut better, leaned back in his chair, propped his crossed feet on his desk and tried to lace his fingers behind his head. He winced when his bruised ribs gave him a nasty reminder stitch, frowned and rubbed the nagging ache that was driving him nuts.

So was having Rockie in his house. He didn't like it any more than she did. She'd made that crystal clear to Max before he'd left for New York, standing flat-footed in the kitchen with her hands on her hips demanding to be taken along.

"I won't be left behind in this backwater of nowhere," she'd declared, "while you go off looking for my father."

"I'm not going looking for your father," Max replied unperturbedly. "I'm going looking for Winston Kimball."

"I can help you," she'd retorted, a pleading edge in her voice. "I'm a whizbang researcher. Gimme a computer and a data base and I'll dig up enough dirt on Winston Kimball to bury him six feet under."

"I work alone," Max told her simply. "But I'll get you that computer."

Which he did before he'd left Thursday afternoon. Sheridan had set it up for her on the oak Shaker table in the dining room. She'd spent the rest of the day playing computer games with a pouty frown on her face and soap operas blaring on the TV in the adjacent living room.

Sheridan had been holed up in his study at the end of the hall for most of the last twenty-four hours. He'd gone through four rolls of fax paper collecting data and seismograph printouts on the Mojave quake. He'd read so many printouts his eyes felt like a seismograph needle jumping across a graph sheet.

On paper it looked like a normal quake, but he knew it wasn't. So far, he was the only one who knew, thank God. The aftershocks the TAQ box had set off had pretty much covered its tracks. Addison had gotten lucky—this time, anyway.

His rolltop desk, computer work center and the two tables that were flush against it, making a squared-off U around three walls, were piled with seismograph printouts and at least a hundred pounds of reference books. None of them had given him any clue as to how the damn thing worked. Neither had the disks they'd taken from Addison's office.

The disks contained Addison's identification of and hunt for Winston Kimball. The search seemed to confirm Rockie's conviction that Addison hadn't known what Kimball had up his sleeve for the TAQ box. For her sake, Sheridan was glad.

Every meeting, every phone conversation, Addison had ever had with Greer Hanlon was recorded, along with a detailed tally of the amount Kimball had invested in the TAQ box and how Addison had spent it.

But there was nothing—zip, zero, zilch—about the TAQ box itself. No schematic, no specifications—absolutely no files pertaining to it at all.

He suspected they were there, since the number of megabytes available indicated *something* was there, but he'd be damned if he could find them. They were probably on a subdirectory he couldn't tap unless he got lucky and guessed what Addison had named it. So far he'd struck out.

"You couldn't find your pants if they were on fire. It can't be that difficult," Rockie had retorted disgustedly when he'd told her. "Dad left the disks for me to find. He wouldn't have made them impossible to figure out."

It was their third knockdown, drag-out argument since Max had left them alone scarcely twenty-four hours ago; the second one had been about the volume of the TV. They'd waged the battle of the disks over a sumptuous dinner of tomato soup and bologna sandwiches the night before. It ended with Rockie insisting the TAQ box specs had to be on the disks, and Sheridan inviting her to go to hell and find it.

She'd spent Thursday evening scrolling through the reams of data on the disks, a determined set to her jaw. He'd spent it scrubbing mustard out of the shirt he'd had on when she'd thrown her sandwich at him.

At least it wasn't a left hook, he thought, rubbing the sore spot on his right arm where he'd found four knuckle-shaped bruises in the shower the day before. She packed a helluva wallop, Wexler's kid, with a helluva lot more than her fist. With her big green eyes, gutsy I-dare-you determination and her sexy little black combat boots.

And her cigarettes. The cause of their first argument, which had commenced within five minutes of Max's leave-taking, when Sheridan told her she couldn't smoke in his house.

"Just where am I supposed to smoke, then?" she'd demanded, hands still on her hips, her weight thrust on her right.

He'd smiled and thumbed toward the double set of solarium doors in the living room that led outside to the brick patio. She'd followed his gaze, her mouth dropping open at the lazy flakes of snow drifting out of the pewter gray sky onto the two inches or so already on the ground.

"But it's snowing!" she'd howled.

"It does that in the winter in the backwater of nowhere."

"Fine." She'd glared at him, eyes narrowed, the buckles and chains on her biker jacket flying as she'd flung it on. "It's your house, Larry Hagman."

Had he mentioned her repertoire of snappy comebacks? He'd watched her sweep snow off a black wrought-iron chair with the cuff of her jacket and plunk down on it, huddled, shivering and inhaling. His mouth had watered just watching her draw smoke. He'd damn near followed her and grabbed the cigarette out of her hand. It was that or yank her to her feet and get his nicotine fix secondhand in a kiss.

He still wanted to, God help him, wanted to rip up the seismograph tapes, stalk down the hall to the spare room where she was sound asleep under a pile of down quilts on the futon—even though it was damn near noon—and kiss her silly. He'd wanted to since he'd first laid eyes on her. He'd wanted to even when he found out who she was.

If it had been anybody but Maxwell, Sheridan would have insisted he take Rockie with him. Forty-eight hours in the constant company of other human beings was about all Max could take. Sheridan knew that—and why—so he hadn't squawked.

But he was beginning to wish he had, beginning to wish he'd never gone to Barstow. He didn't like finding out that Addison Wexler was still stuck in his craw, or that his daughter could see right through him with her big green eyes, past his carefully constructed I'm-just-a-regular-guy facade.

She knew damn good and well he wasn't your Average Joe on the street, but then, neither was she. Maybe that's why he was so transparent to her. Birds of a feather and all that jazz. Not that the why or the how mattered. She had his number and it shook him, brought all the insecurities he'd thought no longer plagued him to the surface and made him seethe with envy.

"How do you do it?" he longed to ask her. "How do you manage to look and act so goddamned average?"

He was pretty sure he knew the answer. Still, he wanted to hear her say it. Like Sheridan, she had perfect SAT scores. The difference was she'd taken the college prep tests at age seventeen—he'd taken them at age eleven. Her parents had let her be normal, his parents hadn't. They'd been so proud of him, the little genius they'd created. He'd been so eager to please them and escape into the math problems he'd been able to solve in his head since his sixth birthday, it hadn't dawned on him—or his parents—that jumping from fifth grade to college was the kiss of death for his social and emotional development.

He'd never fit in. Not ever, not anywhere. He'd been light-years ahead of his MIT classmates, who'd hated him for blowing the grade curve. Kids his age called him a geek, so he'd done everything he could think of to prove he wasn't. Started smoking, grown his hair, worn an earring, even joined the navy after he'd finished his second doctorate at eighteen. He would've had his chest tattooed, too, if Max hadn't dragged him out of the parlor in San Diego by his pierced ear.

Max pulled strings and got him transferred to Intelligence. He'd thrived there, learned how to channel rather than stifle his impulsive streak. He'd been happier than he'd ever been, until the Pentagon had dangled their ultrasecret research and development program and the chance to work with Addison Wexler under his nose. Grabbing it was the biggest mistake he'd ever made—next to going to Barstow.

Much as he wanted to tell Max to shove Addison Wexler and the TAQ box sideways, he couldn't. He owed Nevin Maxwell what little sanity he had, he owed it to himself, since he'd created the goddamn thing, to get the TAQ box away from Kimball before he could do God only knew what else with it, and he owed Rockie an apology for behaving like an absolute jerk from the moment he'd met her.

He heard the toilet flush down the hall, swung his feet off the desk and spun his chair toward the computer. By the time he heard her sleep-shuffled step in the uncarpeted hallway, he was scanning the latest batch of seismograph reports onto the CD-ROM hard drive.

"Any luck?" she asked.

"Not yet."

He could see her yawning in the reflection of the desk lamp. She leaned in the doorway scratching her head, the Southwest Missouri State University sweatshirt he'd given her to sleep in sloping off one shoulder and hanging to the knees of the black leggings she wore. His sweat socks sagged around her ankles and drooped off her toes like elf shoes that had lost their curl.

"Is it still snowing?"

"Nope. It's sleeting."

"God, I *hate* Missouri," she muttered grumpily. "Why do you live here, anyway?"

Sheridan checked the impulse to say, "Just to piss you off." He wasn't going to act like the developmentally arrested dweeb she made him feel like. Not anymore. Not if he could help it.

"I was born in Springfield," he told her. "My parents live here. I like it here."

She said, "Oh," and turned out of the doorway.

Sheridan listened to her pad down the hall toward the kitchen, took his hand off the scanner and wiped it on his jeans. Then he stored the data he'd just copied, put the monitor on screen save and stood up, determined to go apologize and get it over with.

The only problem was he had no idea how to say he was sorry. He wasn't good at apologies. Especially apologies to women. The few he'd attempted had blown up in his face, like all his relationships. Maybe he'd tell her she brought out the worst in him, that she'd caught him off guard at a bad moment.

Or maybe he should tell her the truth. He had lots of acquaintances, but only one friend. He'd slept with his fair share of women, but he'd never had a lover. He should tell her he'd never had a guest before because he liked being alone in his house. It was the one place in the world he didn't have to pretend to be less than he was. He could balance his checkbook in his head and answer all the questions on "Jeopardy!" without somebody calling him a wise-ass.

He wanted to tell her he didn't give a damn who her father was, that she was the first woman with beautiful eyes he'd ever met he didn't have to talk to in simple sentences. He wanted to tell her he was sick and tired of being alone, that he desperately wanted to take turns solving the puzzles on "Wheel of Fortune" with her before Vanna turned over the first vowel.

He wanted to tell her he could make love in French, that she wouldn't know the meaning of the word orgasm until she heard him roll the *R* in Rochelle with his tongue in her ear. The image shot him with chills and gave him courage enough to head for the kitchen before it faded and he lost his nerve.

Halfway down the hall, Sheridan decided he should probably warn her he was out of his mind, too, absolutely, positively out of his ever-lovin' mind to think that maybe, just maybe, she might be attracted to him.

But he was pretty sure she already knew.

14

WHAT ROCKIE KNEW was that if she didn't get a decent meal pretty damn quick she was going to eat Sheridan's socks. It would serve him right for making her feel as welcome as a cockroach. The jerk.

She didn't want to be here any more than he wanted her here, but Maxwell hadn't given either of them a choice. She couldn't smoke in his house, which was fine—it was *his* house, after all—but she'd be damned if she'd starve in it.

The kitchen was well stocked, which surprised Rockie until she found a note stuck to the refrigerator with a ceramic magnet shaped like a pineapple.

Sherry, dear,
The stuff I put in your fridge is called food. Eggs come from chickens, sausage comes from hogs and biscuits come from the bakery—not from McDonald's. Read the cookbook I gave you for Christmas three years ago. If you're smart enough to graduate MIT at 15, you're smart enough to follow a recipe. Because I'm your mother and I'm supposed to do things like this, I took all the pizzas out of your freezer. They are not food. They are microwavable cardboard. I'll give them back, but only if you promise to come for dinner on Sunday.

Love, Mom.

P.S. I took your laundry home with me. I'll bring it back Friday when I'm through at the hospital.

Eleanor Sheridan was a doctor, a cardiologist. Rockie knew because Maxwell had told her. He'd also told her Sheridan's father was a federal judge. She had no idea why he'd told her, she hadn't asked.

"Well, you know what they say, Sheridan. If it isn't one thing, it's your mother." Rockie opened the fridge and helped herself. "What I'd like to know is why she named you Leslie if she calls you Sherry?"

"Because it's my grandfather's name," he said from behind her.

Startled, Rockie dropped an unopened pound of link sausage, gave the fridge door a shove with her hip and turned around. Her arms were loaded with a quart of orange juice, a loaf of bread, a dozen eggs and a tub of butter.

Sheridan leaned on his folded arms on the wood-topped bar that separated the kitchen from the dining room. He hadn't shaved, he had circles under his eyes, and his goofy-looking glasses were stuck on top of his head; still, he was one handsome pain in the ass. The front of his faded black sweatshirt read If You Don't Like Geology, Upper Jurassic.

"Well, that phrase certainly suits your personality." Rockie slid her armload on the countertop next to the stove and picked up the sausage. "Where's the frying pan?"

"Drawer beneath the oven." Sheridan caught the leg of a stool with his foot, tugged it behind him and sat down.

Rockie dropped to her heels and yanked the drawer open with a screech that set his teeth on edge. She came up a second later with a cast-iron skillet, cocked in her hand at an angle that suggested she'd like to clobber him with it.

"Make you a deal," he said. "Scramble me a couple eggs and I'll let you smoke in the house."

"Upper Jurassic." She banged the skillet on the electric burner and gave him a look that would fry eggs. "Spatula?"

"Drawer behind you next to the fridge."

She turned away to get it. Sheridan wiped a hand over his mouth. This was going right into the toilet. He tried smiling when she came back to the stove, but she looked only at the sausage as she opened the package, forked half a dozen links into the skillet and turned on the burner.

"We made headlines again," he said. "Or rather, you did. You and Addison. Want to see the paper?"

"No, thank you. I saw myself on CNN last night. Cups?"

"Cabinet above you on the left."

She took down two, filled them from the pot she'd already brewed and put one in front of him with a spoon, the sugar bowl and a pint of nondairy creamer. All without looking at him. He couldn't decide if she was trying to ignore him or keep him from noticing her puffy, mascara-smudged eyes.

"Thanks. How'd you sleep?"

"Fine." Rockie took a bowl out of the cabinet she'd found the cups in and cracked eggs into it.

She'd rather eat the shells than tell Sheridan she'd lain awake crying until the snow drifting past the window was a watery blur in the glow of the streetlight. She had lots of reasons to cry, but tears never solved anything. And neither did Sheridan, she thought, remembering the disks.

"If the futon isn't comfortable," he said, "you can have my bed tonight."

"I said I slept just fine," Rockie retorted, beating the eggs into a froth with a wire whisk.

"Then how come you look like hell?"

The doorbell rang just as Rockie opened her mouth. Sheridan sprang toward the door, whipping his gun out from under his sweatshirt.

"It's your mother with your laundry," Rockie told him. "Didn't you read her note?"

"Which one? She leaves them around here by the dozen. Besides, she has a key." Sheridan sidled up to the door, peered through the small window cut into it, then glanced at Rockie as he reached behind him and reholstered his gun. "It's my teaching assistant. Duck down the hall."

Rockie switched off the burner and scooted across the dining room. She lost a sock halfway, just as Sheridan threw the dead bolt. She bent to pick it up, heard the door scrape open, left it and sprinted into the hallway.

"Good morning, Dr. Sheridan. I hoped you'd made it home on schedule. This package was delivered express to your office this morning. I thought it might be important."

"Thanks, Connie. For the umpteenth time my name is Leslie, not Dr. Sheridan. Okay?"

"Okay—Leslie."

Rockie heard the breathy, be-still-my-heart catch in Connie's voice. She'd made the same kind of what-ahunk warble when she'd met Mel Gibson at a premiere in L.A.

"I graded the finals last night. I have them here in my briefcase. I'm sure you'll want to double-check them."

"Not today. Leave them in my office and I'll look them over on Monday."

"Oh. Well, all right." Connie's voice throbbed with disappointment. "Afternoon classes are canceled because of the weather. The streets are getting slick, but I guess I can double back and—"

"Never mind. C'mon in."

Big mistake, Sherry, Rockie thought. You blew it when you said call me Leslie.

"I'll just be a minute," Connie said brightly. "I know you're tired and I'll bet you'd like to unpack and—oh, what a lovely house!"

"Thanks."

Rockie grinned at the underwhelmed tone of Sheridan's voice. She heard the door shut, Connie stamp snow on the rug near the threshold, the bump of her briefcase on the table.

"Oh, a loft," she said. "How charming."

Connie stepped into Rockie's sight, her back to her, her head raised to gaze up the ladder at the slanted, beamed-ceiling room that lay in shadow above the living room. The shoulders of her navy peacoat, the red knit cap she tugged off and her pale but colorless curly hair glistened with melting snow.

"Is that—your bedroom?"

"Everybody's got one," Sheridan replied.

"Dean Simmons said you built the house yourself."

"I designed it. I'm a geologist, not a carpenter."

Connie laughed and turned away from the ladder, giving Rockie a profile view of an upturned nose, curved cheek and near heart failure when she glanced down and saw the sock she'd lost. Just leave it there, Rockie willed, but Connie didn't. She bent and picked it up, turned her head to look at the stone fireplace in the living room, swung around to face Sheridan, and froze as her gaze locked on Rockie.

It was only for a second, just long enough to register that the silhouette backed against the shadowed hallway wall was female. Rockie saw it in her pale blue eyes, in the stricken, reflexive blink of her colorless lashes, and she wanted to disappear.

The look on Connie's pleasantly pretty face said she wanted to die, but she gamely lifted her chin as she tore her gaze away, flipped the sock over one of the ladder-backed chairs at the dining room table and stepped out of Rockie's sight. This isn't what you think, Rockie wanted to tell Connie, but she couldn't. She wasn't supposed to be here, she wasn't supposed to be anywhere. All she could do was close her eyes, lean her head against the wall, listen to Connie spring the locks on her briefcase and feel for her.

"Here are the exams, your mail and your messages."

Rockie heard paper slap wood, locks snap and Connie's voice quaver.

"Thanks," Sheridan said. "I appreciate you stopping by, Connie. I really do. You're a great assistant. The best I've ever had."

Don't patronize her, Rockie wanted to shout at him. She didn't think he meant to, she thought he was trying to be kind. That Sheridan was capable of compassion not only amazed Rockie, it incensed her. Oh, I get it now, she thought furiously. He isn't a pain in the ass all the time, just with me.

"There's an assistant professorship opening up fall semester," Sheridan said to Connie. "I'd like to talk to you about it. Maybe we could have lunch sometime."

"Thank you," she replied coolly. "I'd be happy to discuss it, but I'd prefer to do so in your office."

Atta girl, Rockie cheered, tiptoeing down the hall to peek around the corner. Sheridan stood with his hand on the doorknob; Connie stood with her cap on, her coat buttoned and her briefcase in hand.

"Fine," Sheridan said. "At your convenience. Be careful driving home."

"I will. Good day, Dr. Sheridan."

He opened the door and Connie stepped outside. A gust of sleet billowed into the house behind her. Most of the crystals melted on contact, the rest skittered across the hardwood floor as Sheridan flung the door shut and spun toward Rockie as she stepped into the dining room.

"Did she see you?"

"Of course she saw me. I'm not invisible."

"Did she see your *face?*"

"So what if she did?"

"It's on the front page of the newspaper, that's what." He snatched the *News-Leader* off the bar and tossed it on the table where she could see it.

"My mother wouldn't recognize me from that picture."

"You better goddamn hope so." Sheridan grabbed his battered brown bomber jacket off the back of the dining room chair where he'd hung it the night before and yanked the door open. "Hey, Connie!"

Through the open miniblinds on the dining room window, Rockie saw her open the door of a brown Toyota parked at the curb. She was already shivering with cold.

"Leave your car!" Sheridan shouted over the wind moaning under the eaves. "I'll drive you home!"

Rockie sensed more than saw Connie's hesitation. It lasted the two seconds it took Sheridan to step partway outside and pull on his jacket. Then she smiled like the sun had just come out, nodded and shut the car door. Every scrap of compassion Rockie felt for her vanished.

"I hate this goddamn job." Sheridan stepped back inside and kicked the door shut, knocking a picture of a broken-down Model T Ford on the wall beside it cockeyed.

"Which one?"

"Both." Sheridan swiped his Cubs hat off the bar, jammed it on his head on top of his glasses, picked up the express pouch and stuffed it inside his bomber. "If my mother comes by with my laundry, tell her—" He stopped, jerked off his hat, then his glasses, put the cap back on and tossed his glasses on the bar. "I don't care what you tell her. You're an actress. Improvise."

"Is that what you're going to do? Improvise?"

"If necessary." Sheridan avoided her eyes and zipped up his jacket.

"Why don't you drop the cloak-and-dagger stuff? If you want to go neck with your girlfriend, just say so and go."

"I'd love nothing better, next to throwing you on the first plane out of here." Sheridan shoved his hands into brown leather gloves and glared at her. "That's exactly what I would do, and I'd let Connie tell every FBI agent in the country that Rockie Wexler is alive and well in Springfield, Missouri, if only the FAA let planes take off in sleet storms and I didn't have to live in this town when you're gone. But I do, so I have to go do this."

"Not on my account, you don't," Rockie shot back.

"I just said that," Sheridan retorted, wheeling toward the kitchen.

Rockie darted around the table and cut him off. "Are you just gonna leave me here all by myself?"

The thought made her palms sweat. A sure sign of stress-induced dependency. She'd asked Maxwell more or less the same question before he'd left for New York. "Greer Hanlon isn't stupid," he'd told her. "He took a shot at you in L.A. and missed. He won't repeat it. Besides, the best place to hide is in plain sight."

"You're not all by yourself." Sheridan yanked her to the window and pointed at a blue van parked two houses away on the opposite side of the street. "There's an electronics whiz kid named Perry in that van. He's got the phones tapped in case Greer Hanlon calls again. He'll keep an eye on you."

Sheridan fished his keys out of his pocket and headed for the kitchen. When he opened the door that led to the garage, Rockie wheeled after him.

"So what am I supposed to do while you're gone?"

Sheridan glanced at her over his shoulder, the flecks in his jasper eyes flashing. "Smoke in the house," he said, then ducked into the garage and slammed the door.

This time the picture hit the floor.

15

SO DID ROCKIE'S HEART. Metaphorically, anyway. I won't look, she told herself. I won't, I won't—

Her resolve lasted until she heard the garage door go up and a throaty, eight-cylinder engine fire up. Then she gritted her teeth and raced to the window.

"The *hell* I won't," she said fiercely, watching Sheridan back a red Ford pickup with a dark Plexiglas camper shell into the street.

He flipped on the headlights and the wipers, stopped the truck next to Connie's Toyota and got out to help her up into the cab. The radiant expression on her face made Rockie's stomach clutch. She imagined Cinderella must have looked at the prince the same way when he put the glass slipper on her foot, and hoped to God her own heart didn't brim in her eyes like that when she looked at Sheridan.

Not that it would do her any good. He couldn't stand her, plain and simple, which was fine, since most of the time she couldn't stand him, either. Still, she wished he'd smile at her, really smile at her, just once more like he had in L.A.

He didn't look back, didn't so much as glance at the house as he rounded the nose of the truck and climbed in behind the wheel. Rockie watched the pickup truck surefooted as a husky head down the block, past the blue van and turn left at the stop sign. Then she rehung the picture, put on her sock and flipped on the TV and CNN.

She listened from the kitchen for any news about her father while she finished cooking breakfast and ate. Then she washed the dishes and lit a fire. It was cheery and helped take some of the chill off the house. She lit a cigarette, turned down the volume on the TV and rummaged in the cup cupboard until she found an ashtray made from a hollowed-out geode. She had no idea why a man who wouldn't let her smoke in his house kept ashtrays.

While she turned on the computer Maxwell had brought for her and waited for the system to load, Rockie flipped through the mail and messages Connie had delivered. Nothing from her father, but it never hurt to check. The express package was gone. She remembered Sheridan had taken it with him and wondered why.

Rockie rubbed out her cigarette, brought up the list of files she'd copied from her father's diary disks and studied them for the zillionth time. Last night she'd read all the files looking for clues, a code or another directory. She'd peeked over Sheridan's shoulder often enough the day before to know he'd been searching for a hidden subdirectory, too.

Rockie was sure there had to be one. The diary disks were the only place her father would feel safe enough to record the specifics on the TAQ box. Now all she had to do was figure out what he'd named the directory that held the files.

Puffing on another cigarette, Rockie tried to think like her father, and not about Sheridan. At the directory prompt, she typed Rockie, hit Enter and frowned at the INVALID DIR message. She tried Rochelle, her middle name Elaine, Smith, Kimball, the words *quake, TAQ box, tremor* and umpteen others. She tried every possibility that came to mind, no matter how crazy or far out, only vaguely aware of the fax machine in Sheridan's office ringing and receiving almost nonstop while she worked. She found a scratch pad and filled several sheets, keeping track of everything she entered, all with the same result—INVALID DIR.

I'm not thinking convoluted enough, Rockie decided, stubbing out yet another cigarette she'd lit and let burn down to the filter, unsmoked. She stood up and stretched, rolled her cramped shoulders and glanced at the wall clock in the kitchen. Two forty-five.

Had Sheridan taken Connie to lunch to talk about the assistant professorship, or straight to bed? Was he whispering to her about class schedules and tenure over cutesy polka-dot sheets in her frilly, prissy little bedroom?

The image made Rockie feel sick and shaky. She pushed it away, walked to the window, spread two of the blind slats and saw that the sleet had changed back to snow. Another couple of inches had drifted out of the lowering gray sky, bringing the total on the ground close to four, packing the street and dusting the blue van parked on the opposite curb with white.

The street lamps winked on while she stood there rubbing her tired neck muscles. They lightened some of the storm gloom, but not her mood. She gave up trying to think like her father and decided to take a shower to clear her head.

While the hot spray beat on her shoulders, Rockie went over everything that had happened in the last four days. She tried to keep her thoughts focused on the possible significance of the few things her father had had time to do before Conan grabbed him, but her mind kept flashing her pictures of Sheridan.

Her first glimpse of him on the hill above the lab, their god-awful ride down the chute, the smile he'd given her in the car in L.A. The images were sharper and more detailed in memory: the tight fit of his dusty jeans, the muscles she'd felt when he pulled her into the V of his thighs and hooked his legs around hers, the amused, I-almost-like-you twinkle in his jasper eyes when he'd smiled at her.

At the hospital in Barstow her knuckles had brushed his chest when she'd given him the Cubs hat. The memory made her stomach flutter. She wondered if Connie's head was pillowed on his naked chest, if she was gripping the backs of his lean, strong thighs—the images came with a suddenness that sent the bar of soap she was lathering spurting out of her hands.

Rockie picked it up, closed her eyes and swallowed hard. This was sick. What Sheridan did with Connie was none of her business, had nothing to do with her. Feeling sorry for herself wouldn't help her find her father.

She felt better by the time she'd dried off and put on the other outfit Maxwell had bought her, lime green leggings and a lightweight ribbed sweater. It wasn't her color, but with Maxwell leaning against a wall of the boutique he'd taken her to in Barstow with his left arm folded over his right so he could look at his watch without trying, she'd only had time to grab, not shop.

Wait a minute. Rockie switched off the blow dryer she'd found on a linen closet shelf and pursed her lips at her reflection in the mirror over the sink. Her father had been adamant that she call Maxwell the instant she hung up the phone. Maybe his name was the key.

Leaving the blow dryer on the vanity, Rockie darted out of the bathroom and into the hall past Sheridan's study. The fax machine rang again as she passed. She caught a glimpse of the CNN headline news and an offshore oil rig spraying a fountain of raw crude into a cloudy gray sky as she sat down in front of the computer. First she typed Maxwell and hit Enter, gritted her teeth at the INVALID DIR message, then she entered Max and muttered "Damn it" as the message was repeated.

Sitting back in her chair, Rockie tapped the knuckles of her right hand against her chin. There was only one other name she hadn't tried.

"What the hell," she said, typed Sheridan and hit Enter.

The monitor blinked and flashed a new screen—

DIR C:/SHERIDAN/

Gooseflesh raced through Rockie as she read the file list:

APPLICA1	MYNOTES3	SHERRY2
APPLICA2	READFIRST	SPECS
MYNOTES1	SCHEMATIC	WINKIM1
MYNOTES2	SHERRY1	WINKIM2

"Holy-moly," she breathed, a light-headed rush of elation and dread shooting through her.

With shaking fingers, Rockie reached for her cigarettes with one hand, moved the cursor to READFIRST with the other and pressed Enter. A letter addressed to Sheridan, dated Tuesday, November 6, came up. Her cigarettes slipped out of her fingers and tumbled to the floor as she read:

Dear Sherry
You were right about the TAQ box and I was wrong. I wish to God I'd listened to you, but when did I ever listen to anybody?

By now I'm sure you know I copied all your notes before I turned them over to the MPs who rescued us from the island. I'm sorry I took them, that I didn't let them sink to the bottom of the Pacific. Sorrier than you'll ever know.

I'm returning them to you in the files named SHERRY1 and SHERRY2. My notes, the specifications and schematic for the two TAQ box prototypes I built from your design are in the files so named. I'm counting on you to destroy them once you're finished with them, and on you and Maxwell to stop Winston Kimball, my benefactor on the project, before he can implement his plans for the TAQ box. Since I won't be around to help you, see the files named WINKIM1 and WINKIM2 for details.

I've fed Kimball bits and pieces all along, just enough to keep him writing checks. Three months ago, he started dictating alterations to the prototypes. Guesses, really, but near enough to confirm my suspicion that he'd brought in someone else to duplicate and check my work. I thought it was you, until I realized what Kimball has in mind for the TAQ box.

He holds the leases on a number of wells in North Africa, vast deposits that would give him control of the world market, if only they weren't too deep to drill. Based on the changes he demanded in the prototypes, I'm certain he intends to use the TAQ box to trigger a series of small quakes designed to dislodge the deposits and bring them closer to the surface. A brilliant plan on paper. Extremely risky, possibly catastrophic in practice. See the files named APPLICA1 and APPLICA2, short for APPLICATIONS, for particulars.

I confronted Kimball with my suspicions on the phone yesterday, the first time I ever spoke to him, and I hope to God the last. I expected him to deny it and threaten me—which he did—particularly when I told him I was finished with him and the TAQ box. But I didn't expect him to threaten my daughter.

You know I don't frighten easily, but his threats against Rockie scare the hell out of me. She knows nothing about the TAQ box. I told Kimball so, but I don't think he was listening. She's in Spain at the moment. I'd like to think that's far enough out of harm's way, but I'm worried. I left a message for her to call Maxwell when she comes home in two weeks, but I'm not sure she'll do it—she can be as stubborn as I am—or that Kimball won't have a couple of thugs waiting for her at the airport.

Please don't let anything happen to Rockie. Please take care of her for me. She's the best thing I've ever done in my life. I wish I'd had the chance to tell her that myself.

You were a fool to trust me, Sherry, but I was a bigger fool to trust Winston Kimball. May God help us both.

Addison Wexler

16

ROCKIE STARED at the cursor blinking in the middle of the letter, too stunned to cry, too stricken to move. She could hardly breathe, let alone think. The fax machine in Sheridan's office rang again.

It jerked her out of her daze and made her blink and look up. Over the top of the monitor she could see the TV in the living room. The taped, daylight footage rolling across the screen above the banner reading London, England, showed burst water mains flooding Piccadilly Circus and a hairline crack in the dome of St. Paul's Cathedral.

When the tape cut to live satellite feed and a reporter in a gray trench coat, backlit by a battery of klieg lights illuminating a drizzly night sky and the fissured courtyard of Buckingham Palace, Rockie leapt out of her chair and raced for the television. A round oak coffee table sat in the curve of the low beige sectional separating the living room and dining room. She fell over both of them to snatch the remote control off the set and turn up the volume.

"Nothing of this magnitude has struck London since the blitz of World War II," the reporter was saying into his microphone, "and though only minor injuries and damage have been reported from the 4.2 earthquake that rattled the British capital only seconds after Big Ben chimed 2:00 p.m. this afternoon, Londoners are shaken and scientists are baffled."

Rockie was, too, until the aerial view she'd seen earlier, of an offshore oil platform spouting raw crude like a geyser, appeared on the screen.

"This North Sea well owned by Kimball Oil Corporation," the reporter continued, "was scheduled to be shutdown and dismantled—until shortly before 2:00 p.m. this afternoon when the gusher you're seeing now erupted. Anchored off the eastern coast of Scotland, the rig is approximately twenty nautical miles east-southeast of the epicenter of the earthquake that struck London only minutes later.

"The well was successfully capped shortly after this footage was shot from a Royal Navy helicopter on a routine training flight. The oil slick has already been contained and is expected to have minimal impact on nearby fishing banks. British environmentalists are praising the platform crew for their quick action in avoiding a major oil spill in the North Sea."

Rockie stumbled onto the couch, only dimly aware of the nasty throb in her right shin where she'd whacked into the table. Of course the crew moved like lightning, she thought, they were expecting the well to blow. Sheridan had said if her father was smart he'd play along. She hoped he'd set the TAQ box to trigger the quake with a gun to his head, but after reading his letter to Sheridan, she had her doubts.

He'd claimed not to know what Kimball had up his sleeve, but Rockie couldn't buy it. He'd stolen Sheridan's work and admitted it. From there, it wasn't much of a stretch to believe he'd known exactly what he was doing for Winston Kimball and why. Conan had said as much.

Rockie dropped the remote on the cushion beside her and covered her face with her hands. No wonder Sheridan hated her. She'd been prancing around for the last four days extolling the virtues of St. Addison Wexler, the thief, the liar, the cheat—and her father.

The wall phone in the kitchen rang. Rockie raised her head, elbows on her knees and drew a shaky breath. She wanted to cry, or scream, but decided to answer the phone instead. She walked into the kitchen, picked up the receiver on the third ring and said, "Sheridan residence."

"This is Maxwell. Put Sherry on."

"He isn't here. He left a couple of hours ago with his teaching assistant. She saw me. He went with her to talk her out of calling the FBI. I'm sorry."

"Perry, are you on the line?"

"Yes, sir," said a bright, youthful voice.

"I want you in the house with Miss Wexler until Dr. Sheridan returns."

"On my way."

There was a faint click on the line, then Maxwell said, "Something wrong, Rockie?"

Everything, she wanted to say, but couldn't around the lump in her throat. There were tears in her eyes, but she blinked them away and looked into the dining room, at the cursor winking in her father's letter. She could wipe it from the disk and no one but a world-class programmer could ever hope to retrieve it or know it had been there, but that was the kind of thing her father would do.

"I just saw the London quake on CNN," she said, taking a deep breath. "And I found a subdirectory on my father's diary disks. Type Sheridan at the prompt. It's all there. The TAQ box specs and what Kimball plans to do with it."

"Which is?" Maxwell asked.

Rockie told him.

"I'm on my way. I'll find Sherry first and get him back there ASAP," Maxwell said when she'd finished. "You and Perry sit tight."

The line went dead, and the doorbell rang. Rockie hung up the phone, crossed the dining room and opened the door to a shivering, red-faced huddle of quilted black nylon and green knit ski cap.

"Hi, I'm Perry," he said, lifting the baseball bat in his gloved right hand, "and this is Louie."

"Let me guess." Rockie backed away to let him in. "Short for Louisville Slugger."

"You got it." Perry stepped inside onto the rug beside the door and stamped snow off his black Nikes.

A blast of cold came with him, turning Rockie's bare feet to ice and shooting a chill up her spine. Gooseflesh raced up her arms as she shut the door and threw the dead bolt.

"Max keeps telling me I need a gun." Perry waved one hand in front of his face to clear the fog from his gold wire-rimmed glasses and leaned Louie against the wall with the other. "But guns scare the hell out of me."

"Me, too," Rockie agreed feelingly.

"Sure is nice and warm in here." Perry's brown hair crackled with static electricity as he tugged off his ski cap. "Even with a space heater it's damn cold out in that van."

His eyes were brown behind the now-clear lenses of his glasses, his gaze curious but friendly. He wasn't much taller than she was and didn't look old enough to shave, let alone work for Maxwell.

"I'm older than I look," he said. "Honest."

Rockie smiled guiltily. When the fax machine beeped, she nearly jumped out of her leggings. Perry grinned. Sympathetically.

"It's just out of paper." He stuffed his gloves in his pockets, shrugged off his jacket and tossed it over a chair. "I'll reload it."

He toed off his shoes and padded down the hall. Rockie followed him to the spare bedroom, sat down on the unmade futon and tugged on Sheridan's sweat socks.

She'd been freezing ever since she'd set foot in Missouri. She wondered if she'd ever be warm again, and what Sheridan would say when he saw the letter from her father. No wonder he'd wanted to throw her on a plane. She wanted to throw herself in front of one.

On her way down the hall, Rockie stopped in the study doorway. The fax machine was buzzing along again. Perry stood at Sheridan's desk, sorting the slew of faxes that had already been received. When he looked up and saw her, he passed her the first one on the stack.

"This could be trouble," he said.

The U.S. Geological Survey letterhead on the top of the page was a little wavery, but the rest of the message from Dr. Fred Eddings was crystal clear. So was the sharp, angry tone of the five curt paragraphs:

You promised me answers when I let you in on this, Sherry. I want them. And I want them now.

Start with explaining to me why every seismograph station on the planet can pinpoint an epicenter for the quake that hit London, but no underground focus point. Tell me how an earthquake originated on the surface of the North Sea.

Tell me, too, how the secondary seismic wave, which travels 2.05 miles an hour slower than the primary seismic wave, reached that oil platform on the coast of Scotland at the same time. Tell me how secondary waves, which can't move through liquids, managed to zip across a goddamn ocean.

Then explain why the primary wave died when it hit the rig, but the secondary wave didn't. Tell me how in hell it hung a left and followed the coast all the way to London. The damage there screams *S* wave, a side-to-side shake, not an ass over apple roll like a *P* wave.

Tell me, Sherry, that you aren't tinkering with the TAQ box again. Then tell me why I shouldn't call the FBI and the CIA and send them to Springfield to arrest you. Tell me by 9:00 a.m. tomorrow or get your butt on the first plane for Brazil.

Fred

P.S. Be sure you take the TAQ box with you.

"Uh-oh." Rockie's stomach knotted as she passed the fax back to Perry.

"Hope Sherry shows up in time," he replied.

Was the sidelong glance Perry gave her as he laid the fax on the desk accusatory, or was she rapidly developing a colossal guilt complex? Probably both, Rockie decided, ducking quickly out of the doorway and down the hall.

She sat down at the computer, cleared her father's letter and put the monitor on screen save, then went into the living room, retrieved the remote from the couch and shut off the TV. She'd had enough news today to last her a lifetime.

Except for the hum of the hard drive on the computer and the zip of the fax machine, the house was quiet for all of twenty seconds. Then the rumble started. Not inside, but out. Faint at first, then louder as it drew closer. Close enough to rattle the glass pane in the door and send Rockie racing for the dining room window.

It wasn't a tank, it only sounded like one. It was a dump truck, a dented yellow one with a rusty right front fender. A snowplow, she realized, blading the street and flinging salt from the hopper on the rear bumper as it passed.

Just when you think things can't get any worse, they do, Rockie thought, moving to the door to watch the plow. The MPs her father mentioned in his letter meant the government knew about the TAQ box. It might take Uncle Sam a while to put two and two together, but Fred Eddings already had. If they didn't find her father and expose Winston Kimball, Dr. Leslie Sheridan was going to become as infamous as Dr. Victor Frankenstein.

If that happened, she could forget ever seeing Sheridan smile at her again. Unless he managed to get his hands around her throat first.

Rockie leaned her forehead against the frost-rimmed glass in the door and wished she'd stayed in Spain. One look at her naked and the director would have realized he wasn't that desperate. If not a career, she might still have a job. And at least she'd be warm.

At the end of the block, the snowplow turned around to make another pass. Though it was barely four it was nearly dark. A few last flakes of snow fluttered in the plow's headlights as the driver dropped the blade and gunned the engine.

The scrape of metal on ice set Rockie's teeth on edge. The speed at which the plow came sweeping down the street raised the hair on her arms. If this guy doesn't slow down he's going to hit Connie's car, Rockie thought, no more than half a second before the plow veered toward the opposite curb and slammed into the back end of the blue van.

The blade caught the bumper with a grinding shriek and lifted the van off the ground. It shuddered forward a couple of feet on its front wheels before the tires got hung up on the curb and it heaved over on its right side and rolled twice. Hard enough to smash the windshield and flatten the roof.

"Holy shit!" Perry shouted from the study.

Rockie heard him running sock footed down the hall toward her, but was too stunned to move until the cab door opened and the snowplow driver jumped nimbly to the ground. He wore gray thermal overalls and an orange safety vest, had short-cropped brown hair and the biggest hands—

Rockie's heart skidded and her breath caught. It can't be him, she told herself, it can't, it can't. She squeezed her eyes shut, counted three and opened them.

But it was *him*—it was Conan.

He stripped off the vest, tossed it back in the cab, shut the door and started across the street. At an easy, unhurried walk, a smile on his face.

"Max is gonna kill me." Perry slid to a halt beside Rockie, did a double take through the window in the door and swallowed. Hard. "Oh, shit. If Conan doesn't first."

"Smash the computers," Rockie said urgently. "Forget the monitors. Just make sure you pulverize the hard drives."

Perry didn't ask questions, just grabbed Louie, hit a grand slam off the PC on the table, then sprinted toward the study. Hoping to God Sheridan had another set of copies, Rockie grabbed her father's disks off the dining room table, raced into the living room and threw them into the fire. Then she went back to the window in time to see Conan step onto the curb.

"Come and get me, you son of a bitch," she said under her breath, then she spun around and smacked into Perry.

"Get out the back and run." He shoved her boots at her, grabbed her arm and yanked her toward the patio doors.

"No!" Rockie pulled against him and managed to drag both of them to a skidding halt.

"Look, Miss Wexler." Perry tugged her forward another foot or so. "If Conan doesn't kill me, Max will if I let anything happen to you. Louie and I will hold him off."

"You and Louie don't stand a chance." Rockie wrenched free, dropped her boots and gripped his arms. "Conan's boss wants me so he won't hurt me, but if you get in his way he'll kill you. That's a 99.9 percent surety. Somebody has to tell Maxwell what happened to me, and if you're dead, who's going to do that?"

Perry hesitated, biting his lower lip. He was just a kid, no matter what he said, and he was scared. Rockie didn't blame him. She was terrified. His indecision lasted all of two seconds, until a thundering crash hit the front door.

"You're sure he won't hurt you?"

"Positive," Rockie said, hoping to God it was true.

"Okay, I'll go. But next time I'm bringing a gun." Perry ran for the glass doors and pushed the right one open as another blow shook the house.

"Give Sheridan a message for me." Rockie grabbed the door handle behind Perry as he slid outside. "Tell him, C, colon, back slash, Sheridan, back slash. He'll get it."

"Will do." Perry nodded and broke for the chain link fence at the back of the yard.

Rockie watched until he'd vaulted it safely, then shut the door and whirled around, just as the battered front door fell into the dining room with a crash.

Conan stood on the porch, empty-handed and scarcely breathing hard. He'd kicked the door in, Rockie realized, gripping the back of the couch to keep from shaking.

"Hello, Miss Wexler." He stepped into the house, smiling as he moved past the splintered computer and glanced at the disks melting and smoking in the fireplace. "I trust you smashed the system in Dr. Sheridan's study, as well?"

"You bet. Wanna check?"

"No. I believe you. Where's the boy?"

"Long gone," Rockie lied, picking up her combat boots and clutching them to her chest.

"Miss Wexler." Conan looked at her askance. "You should know better."

He started toward her, his gaze lifting past her, searching, toward the patio doors. Rockie stepped in front of him.

"Let him go. He can't hurt you."

Conan lowered his gaze and looked at her. His eyes were like Maxwell's, dead and lifeless, without compassion or remorse.

"Must I remind you that my employer believes in insurance."

"Please," Rockie pleaded. "He's only a kid."

Something flickered in Conan's eyes. For only a moment, hardly more than a heartbeat, then he turned away and swept her biker jacket off the back of a chair.

"Very well, Miss Wexler, for you. But just this once." He held her jacket open for her but didn't smile. "Quickly now. Your father is waiting."

17

IT WAS A TWENTY-MINUTE drive from Connie's place to Sheridan's. Sheridan made it in twelve. If the roads hadn't been icy, he would have made it in ten.

He'd been about to step out of his jeans when Perry called from the 7 Eleven three blocks from his house. He'd zipped up, buckled up, grabbed his bomber and his Cubs hat and raced for the truck with Connie screaming sexual harrassment behind him.

Not that he gave a damn. She'd made it clear what her price was for keeping her mouth shut about Rockie. He'd had two choices—pay up or tie her up and gag her. He'd just figured out he stood a much better chance of cajoling her into a rope with his pants *off* when the phone rang.

He wished he'd listened to his mother. She'd said you couldn't trust a woman who doesn't wear mascara. Or good old Do-Whatever-It-Takes-To-Get-The-Job-Done Maxwell. He would have had Connie on the sheets in five minutes flat and been finished with her in five more.

He should have done the same thing and split. He would have, for the sake of expedience, if only he hadn't been so damn sure he'd never be able to look Rockie in the eye. Now he'd be lucky if he ever saw her again. Period.

The thought scared the hell out of him. So did seeing the totaled blue van being winched onto a tow truck when he made the turn onto his block. He'd kill Conan for this. If it was the last thing he ever did, he'd kill him.

He left the truck in the driveway and ran for the house. The harsh glare of the porch light on the fresh snow and his bashed-in front door, precariously re-hung on its hinges, made him want to kick it down himself. He pushed past it instead and jerked off his cap and his bomber. From the inside pocket, he took the diskette mailer he'd removed from the express pouch Connie had delivered earlier.

Inside were the copies Maxwell had made of Addison Wexler's diary disks. He'd mailed them to himself from Barstow after Max copied them. The disks Rockie had tried to exchange for her father were dupes. Winston Kimball wasn't the only one who believed in insurance. Sheridan hoped Kimball kept his premiums paid. His survivors were going to need it.

He tossed his jacket over a chair, saw Rockie's lighter next to the hollow, ash-filled geode and her cigarettes on the floor under the table. He picked them both up and glanced into the kitchen.

The clock on the microwave read 4:47. Perry said Conan plowed into the van, literally, almost dead on the stroke of four. With a jet and a fifty-minute head-start, he could be an easy five hundred miles away. The direction didn't matter, only his ultimate destination.

He wasn't sure what he'd do if Wexler's disks didn't tell him where that might be, or at least give him a clue. He wasn't going to think about it, either. Not unless—or until—he had to.

"Perry!" Sheridan shouted as he snatched his glasses off the bar. "You got that backup drive connected yet?"

"Just finished," Perry answered, dumping a shattered pile of split plastic casing and dangling components into a corner of the study as Sheridan swung through the doorway.

"Nice job," he said, eyeing what used to be a five thousand dollar, 1200 MG CD-ROM hard drive.

"I can rebuild it, no problem." Perry turned quickly to face him. "Sorry, Sherry. Smashing it seemed like a good idea at the time."

"It wasn't a good idea, Perry, it was brilliant." Sheridan dropped into his swivel chair and fired up the spare hard drive. It wasn't quite as state of the art as the 1200 MG, but it would do. "If Conan had gotten his hands on Addison's files, we could all kiss our asses goodbye."

"It wasn't my idea. It was Miss Wexler's. She burned the disks, too."

Sheridan was surprised. Not that Rockie had thought of it, but at the tone of Perry's voice. God knew he'd had enough hands-on experience with a bent out-of-shape ego to recognize one when he heard it. He fed a disk into the port, hit copy and turned his chair around. "It doesn't matter who thought of it."

"I wussed out, Sherry." Perry sat down on an ottoman that matched a blue upholstered armchair and laid his elbows on his knees. "Miss Wexler said Conan wouldn't hurt her, but he'd kill me, that if I was dead I couldn't tell Max what happened and I should run. So I did."

"She was right." Much as it killed Sheridan to admit it, he couldn't imagine how Rockie must have felt. "You were smart to listen to her."

"Then why do I feel like such a coward?"

If the shoe fits, Sheridan wanted to say, but checked the impulse. He didn't have time for guilt. His or anybody else's. Conan already had a good hour's jump on him.

"I'd put the probability at 97.4 that if you'd tried to stop him, Conan would have used Louie to break every bone in your body. Twice."

"That's what Miss Wexler said. Only she said it was ninety-nine percent."

"Cut her some slack. She doesn't know you and Louie as well as I do."

Oh, boy, did he know Perry. He'd *been* Perry once upon a time. Sheridan could tell him that, but he wouldn't believe him.

"I ought to quit," Perry said miserably.

"Your choice, but do me a favor first. Take my truck and go buy me a pack of cigarettes."

"You don't smoke."

"I do now. Marlboro Reds. Keys are in the ignition." Sheridan took out the first disk and inserted the second. "Make it snappy. I might need a good techno nerd."

"No need to insult me," Perry grumbled. "Remember what Miss Wexler said."

"I remember. Get going."

Perry went. Sheridan lit one of Rockie's cigarettes, leaned back in his chair and waited for the rush. It hit him almost as hard as his first glimpse of her bailing out of her Jeep. She'd been scared to death then, too, but she'd kept her cool. Hopefully, her cigarettes would keep him from losing his until he had his hands around Conan's throat.

While he copied the rest of the disks, he read the fax from Fred Eddings. He wrote an answer when he finished, sent it to Fred at home on the internal modem and received a curt, three-sentence reply on the external machine ten minutes later: I must be crazy, but okay. Three days. Then I call the feds.

It wasn't much time, but it would have to do. He'd make it do, Sheridan vowed, typing C:/SHERIDAN/ at the directory prompt. His jaw clenched when the file list came up. It started to twitch as he read Wexler's letter.

"Aw, hell," he said, wiping a hand over his mouth when he finished.

It was too much to hope that Rockie hadn't read it. He'd planned to tell her himself, had gleefully and maliciously been waiting for just the right moment to drop this little bomb. Until Conan had beat him to it and he'd seen the look on her face.

He wondered what she thought of her father now, what she thought of him, but didn't have time to dwell on it. With every second that passed, Conan got farther away and harder to find. He skimmed the WINKIM files, took notes while he read SCHEMATIC and SPECS, then concentrated on the APPLICA files.

Perry came back with his cigarettes and made coffee. It was almost as lousy as his. Sheridan drank four cups, anyway, and smoked half the pack by the time Max arrived. He was dressed all in black, cords, sweater and bomber, his gaze as brittle as the ice-crusted snow outside.

"Update me," he said to no one in particular.

Sheridan was still at the computer, his back to Perry. He didn't need to see him to know he was shaking.

"Don't fall on your sword," he said. "Just tell him."

Perry did. Sheridan keyed back to the directory, positioned the cursor at the file he wanted and listened.

"I know this guy in the tower at the airport," Perry finished. "A private Gulfstream jet made an unauthorized takeoff at 5:20. Security found an abandoned city plow with blue metallic paint all over the blade in the parking lot about ten minutes later."

"Wonderful." Maxwell shrugged off his jacket, tossed it aside and said, "Winston Kimball and Kimball Oil are squeaky clean. Three subsidiary corporations, however, have dirt under their fingernails. Greer Hanlon is listed as president of one, an oil drilling company in Oklahoma City. I paid him a call today. He left this morning for Egypt. Taking the wife to see the pyramids, his secretary said."

He sat down on the edge of the desk, laid his elbow on his knee and smiled. The smile came closer to his eyes than Sheridan had seen in a long time.

"Now it's your turn, Sherry. What are we up against?"

"Pandora's box." Sheridan wheeled his chair around to face the monitor and brought up the TAQ box schematic.

Max stood up behind him for a better look. Perry joined him and let out a slow whistle.

"You don't need a techno nerd," he said.

"No need to insult me," Sheridan replied, paging down to the next screen. "Looks complex, but the basic principle—"

"Cut to the chase," Max interrupted. "We don't have time for a lecture."

"Wait a sec." Perry reached, pointing, over Sheridan's shoulder. "That's a wave oscillator, right?"

"Gold star," Sheridan said. "My original harebrained idea was to use the oscillator to change the shape of the seismic waves, to flatten them out and speed them up. The big, slow-rolling underground loops they make are what do all the damage in a quake." He scrolled to the next screen, picked up a pencil and used the eraser to point out two intricate-looking components. "These little devils are Addison's addition. He calls them directional locators, but they don't locate a damn thing. Near as I can tell, they stabilize seismic waves and change their direction."

"Yikes," Perry murmured. "Ready, aim and fire."

"More or less," Sheridan said grimly.

"Is that how the secondary wave that struck London today managed to move through water?" Maxwell asked.

"Near as I can figure. I'm guessing Addison was pushing buttons from a Kimball oil tanker anchored twenty nautical miles east-southeast of the offshore well. That's why it looks like the quake started on the surface of the North Sea and why there was no tsunami." Sheridan stood up and rubbed his aching ribs. "I know enough about how the locators work to be dangerous. Gimme twenty-four hours—"

"I don't care how they work. All I want to know is can you disable them?"

"Anybody can. The TAQ box has a built-in self-destruct. Loosen any three bolts on the housing and it automatically fries its own brain. Now look at this."

Sheridan leaned over the keyboard and pulled up another file. A SPECS file, dated October 17, appeared.

"'Lab test of directional locators complete failure,'" Sheridan read. "'Zigged someplace where I should have zagged. Rechecking my equations. Project now eight months behind schedule and five hundred thousand over budget. Smith antsy, bitching about overtime. Next lab test scheduled for 10 November.'"

"That's tomorrow," Perry said.

"Two gold stars. The TAQ box has yet to pass a single lab check, Max, let alone a field test. It has more bugs in it than the Hubble telescope. That's why Addison wiped the mainframe in the lab. He probably meant to destroy the prototypes, too, but Conan surprised him." Sheridan handed him the fax from Fred Eddings. "The USGS picked up on the anomalies in the London quake. I've faxed Fred. He'll give us three days."

"What are the chances Addison didn't know what he was doing? Or Kimball's plans for the TAQ box?"

"That he didn't know what he was doing, nil," Sheridan replied truthfully. "That he knew what Kimball was up to, fifty-fifty," he lied, being generous for Rockie's sake.

"Any idea why Kimball pushed up the timetable?"

"He's running out of time." Sheridan keyed up one last file, a map of the Western Desert, a portion of the Sahara in western Egypt near the Libyan border. "The three flashing red dots indicate leases on wells held by Kimball Oil that are due to expire within the next year."

"Which one do you think they're going to try to blow?"

"All three. They're close enough together. The question is where they're going to try to blow them from."

"Best guess."

Sheridan hated the word, hated to guess. Especially with Rockie's life on the line. A woman he was pretty sure he could fall in love with if they could quit fighting long enough.

"Here. It's an oasis." He used the pencil again to indicate the middle dot. "They'll need water and as much shade as they can get. Even in winter, daytime temperatures are well over a 100°F. There are some handy ruins and tombs, too, that just might give them the underground access they'll need."

"Everybody's passport current?" Maxwell asked.

Sheridan nodded. So did Perry, with an almost imperceptible gulp.

"Be packed and ready to go in an hour." Maxwell picked up his jacket and tossed it over one shoulder. "Let me see if I've got this straight. The TAQ box can change the shape and direction of seismic waves, but it can't generate them."

"Right," Sheridan confirmed, lighting a cigarette.

"That explains Conan's involvement." Maxwell shrugged into his jacket. "See you at the airport."

When the shattered front door groaned shut behind him, Sheridan picked up his coffee cup and headed for the kitchen. Perry followed, looking perplexed.

"How does that explain Conan?" He asked, wrapping himself around a stool while Sheridan helped himself to the last of the coffee.

He looked at Perry through a haze of blue smoke drifting from the cigarette. "What else besides earthquakes generate intense ground movement and seismic waves?"

"Lemme see." Perry bent an elbow and leaned his chin on his fist. "Volcanoes, freight trains, explosives—" He blinked, blanched, and his chin slid off his fist. "You mean Conan sets off a bomb and Dr. Wexler directs the seismic waves it creates?"

"Short of waiting a couple hundred years for Mother Earth to oblige, I can't think of a quicker way to move a fault. What do you think?"

"I think," Perry said, swallowing hard, "I should have quit when I had the chance."

18

BE CAREFUL WHAT you wish for, Rockie's mother used to say, or you just might get it. She'd wished to be warm, so now she was sweltering. Even though it was winter in Egypt and scarcely past noon.

She was still wearing her sweater and leggings, which didn't help. Conan wore the short-sleeve plaid shirt and tan trousers he'd had on under the gray coveralls. He'd shed those at the airport in New York. Before they'd boarded an Air Egypt flight for Cairo, and after he'd given her a pair of gold wire cartouche earrings. Rockie hadn't wanted to take them, but he'd insisted. When she'd put them on, he'd shown her the transmitter in his pocket.

"The earrings carry an electrical charge. Enough to render you breathless and cause you pain should you do something silly like scream. Would you like a demonstration?"

Rockie had declined and walked demurely onto the plane. That was in New York, but now they were in Aswân, walking the last few yards across a broiling runway toward a red helicopter with Kimball Oil painted boldly in white on the tail.

It was not a good sign. It meant there was no longer any need for secrecy or pretense.

"It's my feet," Rockie complained to hide her unease, as Conan leaned past her to open the cockpit door. "Combat boots are cool, but they're not *cool,* know what I mean?"

"Where we're going," he replied unperturbedly, "you'll be glad to have them."

"Oh, yeah? Where's that?"

"Miss Wexler." He looked pointedly down his nose at her. "Please."

"If I didn't ask, you'd be disappointed."

"Actually, I would be grateful."

Rockie almost smiled but caught herself and climbed into the cockpit. She didn't want to know Conan had a sense of humor. It was even scarier than realizing if he could kick his way through a dead bolt she had about as much chance as a snowball in hell of escaping him.

Conan walked around the chopper, got in and fastened his harness, put on a headset and handed Rockie one. She put it on, waited until he'd fired up the engine, then said, "Let me guess. Egyptology is your hobby, and since we're in the neighborhood—"

"I have no hobbies."

"You should get a couple. You wouldn't be so tense."

He glanced her a smile, his eyes invisible behind a pair of sunglasses with mirror lenses. The Terminator in the flesh. Rockie shivered despite the stifling heat and put on the shades Maxwell had bought her in Barstow.

Once they were airborne and whipping across the desert, a bleak, dun landscape that seemed to stretch forever, Conan turned on what he said was the air conditioner and was obviously a joke. Rockie wilted in her seat and tried not to sweat. She might as well have tried not to breathe.

Conan passed her a canteen and his handkerchief. "Drink and bathe your face."

It helped, but not much. She kept the canteen in her lap and one eye on Conan. The chopper skimmed fairly close to the ground, slow enough that it didn't kick up much of a wake. His big hands steady on the stick, he kept watch in all directions.

Making sure they weren't being followed. She should be so lucky, Rockie thought, but it was highly likely her luck had run out. Even if Maxwell had the first clue where to look for her, he might not bother. Sheridan wouldn't, she knew that for sure. She wished she didn't, almost regretted finding the subdirectory.

If Maxwell chose to wash his hands of her—and she wouldn't blame him—maybe he'd turn the disks over to the FBI. Maybe they'd feel inclined to rescue her and her father, but Rockie couldn't see the feds getting real worked up about a thieving, kidnapped scientist. They'd probably figure he deserved whatever he got. If anyone came it would be for the TAQ box, not Addison and Rockie Wexler.

Tears sprang in her eyes, but she blinked them away. Fiercely. Wexlers never quit. She'd escaped Conan once, she'd do it again. Idly, she raised her right hand and stroked the cartouche in her earlobe. It was a conventional wire drop hooked in the back through a half loop. A flick of her thumbnail—

A jolt so sharp it stole her breath sizzled through Rockie. Reflex jerked her hand away so suddenly she nearly ripped the cartouche out of her ear.

"Please don't make me do that again, Miss Wexler. I don't enjoy it. I'm a businessman, not a sadist."

Her heart pounding from the shock and her ear throbbing, Rockie whipped toward him, straining her seat harness. "How can you call what you do a business?"

He turned his head just a fraction to look at her. "I draw a salary for my services. I don't crave fame like your father, nor am I driven by revenge like Dr. Sheridan."

"At least they *feel* something. At least they're human."

Conan smiled. "And what do you think I am?"

"A real unhappy camper," Rockie told him. Why not, she thought. He's going to kill me, anyway. "I think somebody someplace along the line done you wrong. Big time."

"You're very young, Miss Wexler." Conan's smile softened. "And very naive."

"Naive, hell. I live in L.A.," Rockie shot back.

She meant to get a rise out of him, but he merely turned his head and went back to scanning the horizon. So did Rockie. There wasn't much to see, but it was something to do besides think about the fear knotting her stomach.

By the direction of the sun, she gauged they were flying roughly northwest. Over occasional wadis, pebbled stretches and shifting dunes which she mistook for a column of camels until she blinked and realized it was a mirage. They'd been airborne close to two hours, she figured, when the chopper skimmed another slope of sand dunes and she saw an oasis wavering in the distance.

She thought it was another mirage, closed her eyes, counted ten and opened them. It was still there, still shivering in and out of focus, but growing larger and closer with every beat of the chopper rotor.

It stretched a goodly distance near the base of a sandstone escarpment, an impossibly green strip in the midst of a vast depression cupped by dunes. Rockie saw palm trees and tents huddled around them. Two mudbrick buildings squatted near the foot of a jumbled slope crowned by a necropolis of fallen stones and crumbled columns on the northernmost edge of the oasis. As Conan put the chopper down near the tents, she realized it had once been a part of the escarpment, had broken off, probably, in some long-ago earthquake.

How fitting, she thought, turning her attention toward the tents. There were at least a dozen of them clustered near the palms, made of cotton striped in earth tones with fluted sides. Bedouin tents, Rockie realized. Hiding in plain sight, as Maxwell would say.

When Conan cut the engine and climbed out of the cockpit, she did the same. The heat hit her like a fist. So did seeing Gino striding toward them around one of the tents. He wore a sweat-soaked turquoise Gold's Gym tank top, frayed cutoffs and a gauze patch on his left cheek.

"Oh, hell," Rockie said, ducking out from under the rotor. She didn't think Conan heard her over its winddown spin, until he said, "Don't worry, Miss Wexler. He won't hurt you."

"At least not until you tell him," she snapped as they cleared the rotor.

"Welcome to hell, Rockie," Gino said, a nasty smile on his face. "I plan to make your stay here as brief and painful as possible."

He was at least three inches shorter but a good forty pounds heavier than Conan. Still, before Rockie even saw him move, Conan had wound a fistful of Gino's shirt around his hand and hauled him up on his toes.

"Miss Wexler is a guest," he said in his smooth, pleasant voice. "Until you are told otherwise, you will treat her with courtesy. Is that clear?"

"Yeah, it's clear," he gritted between clenched teeth.

Conan let him go. He staggered but managed not to fall. Rockie was disappointed. She would have enjoyed seeing Gino on his duff in the sand.

"Where is Mr. Kimball and Dr. Wexler?"

"Not here yet," Gino said, smoothing his shirt.

Rockie felt a stab of disappointment. She wasn't sure what she'd do when she saw her father. Hug him first, then slug him, probably. Gino's hands, she noticed, were shaking.

"Their flight out of London was delayed. Kimball's new toy ripped up a couple of runways. Hanlon's in Cairo waiting for them. He radioed a while ago. His chopper barely made it. Sand in the engine or something. You're supposed to take this bird back and collect them."

"And so I shall," Conan replied. "Just as soon as I refuel and the radio operator verifies Mr. Hanlon's message."

"I'm not a liar," Gino snarled.

"No, you're a thug, and not a very good one." Conan took Rockie's elbow. "This way please, Miss Wexler."

Rockie could have found the radio operator blindfolded. She didn't see the generators, but she heard them humming outside the largest of the two mud-brick houses. She figured they were hidden behind the crates stacked beneath a canopy strung from the roof.

The smaller hut stood a considerable distance away on the fringe of the oasis. Red-and-white *Explosives* warnings in English and Arabic were nailed to the door, an Arab guard in sweat-stained khakis stood outside with an Uzi.

Another guard opened the door of the big hut when Conan pounded on it. Rockie stepped past him and almost fainted with relief at the blessedly cool air pumping out of the air conditioner cut into one of the table-lined walls. Three men sat in folding chairs monitoring the equipment spread on top of them: four radios, a dozen computers, as many printers and fax machines spitting data and five seismographs. A fourth man in a white lab coat sat with his back to her at a makeshift desk in a far corner.

"Yowza," Rockie said under her breath. Welcome to Mission Control, she thought.

The man at the middle table glanced at them, took off his headset and stood up. Conan walked toward him, leaving Rockie by the door. Praying he didn't have eyes in the back of his head, she raised her right hand to her earring, and froze as the man in the white lab coat turned away from the desk.

It was Rodney Webster, her father's senior lab assistant. He got up and came toward her, hands in his pockets, a hesitant smile on his boyish face. Rockie dropped her hand and made a fist. She intended to flatten his freckled, upturned nose, until she realized he was no better than her father.

"I'm sorry you got dragged into this, Rockie." Rodney stopped in front of her. "I told Hanlon and Kimball you don't know anything, but they didn't believe me."

"I'm insurance, Rod. Kimball believes in it. Guess that's why he bought you."

"It wasn't the money," he retorted angrily. "You don't know what it's like to work for your father. He takes credit for everything. The TAQ box wouldn't work without me. I came up with the directional locators. It was *my* idea, not his, but the great Addison Wexler—"

"If Miss Wexler truly knows nothing," Conan said, stepping up behind him, "let's keep it that way. Shall we?"

Rodney spun on one heel, saw Conan and swallowed hard. He smiled and folded a piece of paper into his shirt pocket.

"Do you carry a sidearm, Mr. Webster?"

"Yes. Yes, I do."

"Let me see it, please."

Rodney fumbled behind him inside his lab coat, fished a gun out of the waistband of his jeans and gave it to Conan. He examined it and gave it back, tucking it securely in the front of Rodney's jeans.

"Carry it here. It does you no good if you can't reach it when you need it. Are you prepared to use it?"

"If I have to. Hanlon warned us about the desert tribes. He said they're great sneak thieves, that we should be on the lookout—"

"I must return to Cairo," Conan interrupted him. "I'm placing Miss Wexler in your care. Make sure she's given a shower, a change of clothes, something to eat and a generous water ration, then keep her in here with you where it's cool. I'll assign you another guard. Any questions?"

"Yeah, one." Rodney swallowed again, his face turning pale. "When will you be back?"

"By nightfall." Conan turned to Rockie. "You may take off the earrings, Miss Wexler."

"I don't understand you." She slipped the cartouches out of her ears and dropped them in his hand. "If Kimball tells you to, you'll shoot me without batting an eye."

"Yes, Miss Wexler, I will. But in the meantime there's no need for you to suffer."

Conan dropped the earrings in his pocket and opened the door. Then he paused and cast a last, chilling look at Rodney over his shoulder.

"If Gino tries to harm Miss Wexler, shoot him. I'll give the guard the same instructions. If you don't shoot him, you'll wish you had."

19

THE DOOR FELL SHUT behind Conan with a dusty whoosh. Rockie heard his voice outside, raised in Arabic, and she released the breath she hadn't realized she was holding.

"Nice company you keep, Rod."

"Don't start, Rockie." Rodney wiped his hands on his lab coat. "Hang on a minute."

He spent more like an hour, maybe an hour and a half, talking to the guy monitoring the seismographs and making notes on a clipboard. While she waited, Rockie sat down on a stack of crates and watched the seismographs. The needles were steady, hardly fluctuating.

Three of the computer monitors displayed infrared photos of rock strata with pools of red between them. The pictures were snowy and skipped a lot. It took her a minute to realize she was looking at oil deposits trapped in shale, ones that were too deep to drill.

Maybe that's what they needed the dynamite for, she thought, lifting her gaze from the monitors as Rodney put down his clipboard and came back to her with a curt "Let's go." A very tall and well-muscled Arab armed with an Uzi stood outside. He followed them at a watchful distance across the camp.

The whole place was put together to look like a Bedouin encampment, from a distance or from the air. The line of hobbled camels was a nice touch. An Arab workman was tossing them grass. Another half-dozen moved busily around the oasis. One was looping a line of fat black hoses and tossing them inside a pavilion-size tent, staked a prudent distance from the camp. The fuel dump, Rockie figured. There was no sign of Gino or the red chopper.

Near the well, a muddy pool ringed by stacked flat stones, stood another good-size tent. The flap was open, a dim bulb glowing inside.

"This is the shower tent," Rodney said. "The water is premeasured to three minutes. Don't drink it. It's clean enough but it tastes like camel dung."

Rockie stepped inside, and he lowered the flap. She found soap and a towel on a wooden bench next to a white cotton gauze shirt and trousers. The shower had a rough board floor and a plastic curtain strung from a wire loop. Stripping quickly, Rockie stepped into it and pulled the chain.

She washed, rinsed and dried and reached for the white shirt. Deodorant, panties, a bra and clean socks tumbled onto the sand. She picked up the underwear and checked the tags. They were her size. Of course, she'd been expected.

Rockie swore under her breath. She'd give them something they didn't expect—just as soon as she thought of it.

Once she'd dressed, she spread the towel on the bench. The shirt had dolman sleeves, hung to her knees and was already stuck to her back. She started toward the flap, finger combing her wet hair. By the time it was dry, she'd look like Little Orphan Annie.

"Drink up." Rodney handed her a large plastic glass of water when she emerged from the tent. "It's bottled."

Rockie drank it in four swallows. It was tepid but delicious. She gave the glass back, fell into step beside Rodney as he started toward Mission Control and nodded at the guard trailing behind them. "Does he speak English?"

"No." Rodney shaded his eyes and watched a small dust cloud moving along the sloping flanks of the escarpment.

"Company coming?" Rockie asked.

"The locals bringing their sheep to water. Hanlon hates it. They're terrible thieves, but he can't keep them off the oasis without starting a bloodbath."

"Hanlon oughta know all about those. He destroyed Dad's lab, Rod. And killed eight of his own men in the process."

"It was an earthquake," Rodney said stubbornly and quickened his pace.

"The hell it was. It was the TAQ box. Conan wired a bomb to one of the prototypes." Rockie grabbed his arm, made him stop and look at her. "I was there, Rod. I saw it."

"Hanlon's a businessman. Why would he do such a thing?"

"Why does he keep Gino around? And Conan? Why all the guns, Rod? Why all the secrecy?"

"Industrial sabotage, Rockie."

"Bullshit, Rodney. My father left a letter admitting he stole the the TAQ box from Sheridan, confessed that he copied his research before the government confiscated the TAQ box as dangerous and irresponsible."

"It isn't dangerous. It passed its field test yesterday in the North Sea, brought in a well that was nearly dry."

"It also triggered a four-point quake in London."

Rodney blinked, stunned. "You're lying."

"Am I? The radio operator has a short wave. Tune in CNN. I'm sure it's still news."

"Hanlon won't let us—" Rodney broke off, looked away from her and dragged a hand through his brown hair. "Shit."

"Don't make the same mistakes my father did, Rod. We can get out of this," Rockie said, hooking her arm through his. "You and me. We can get help—"

"I can't." He pulled away from her. "I'm in too deep."

"Rodney—"

"Back off, Rockie. I mean it."

He hurried ahead of her, dragging a hand through his hair again. Rockie didn't want to, but she let him go. Hopefully she'd planted enough seeds to sprout a healthy crop of doubt, one she could harvest before nightfall, when Conan came back with Hanlon, Winston Kimball and her father. If she wasn't here they couldn't use her against him. Somehow, some way, she had to get out of here by sunset.

Rodney stopped outside Mission Control and waited for her. When she caught up, he nodded toward a nearby palm, said something to the guard in Arabic and followed Rockie into the thin patch of shade.

"I told him you wanted to see the sheep come in," he said. "Let's say you're right. Who'd believe us?"

"The USGS, for starters." Her heart racing with excitement, Rockie screened her eyes and turned to watch the dust cloud spilling down the slope toward them.

"They picked up on the anomalies in the London quake."

She gave him a synopsis of Fred Eddings's fax to Sheridan and everything that had happened since Tuesday. By the time she'd finished, Rodney was frowning. In the distance, Rockie could make out woolly little bodies in the dust.

"The directional locators are still haywire. They flunked their lab tests. I told Addison how to fix them, spent two whole weeks ironing out the glitch, but he's so damned determined to be right, to do everything his way."

So were the sheep, Rockie noticed, listening to Rodney carp about her father. It was an old topic, so she tuned him out and thought about means of transport as she watched the men on horseback herd the sheep out of a wadi. There were maybe forty in the flock and half as many riders, swathed in dark, loose robes and headdresses with one corner drawn over their mouths to keep out the dust.

"Where's the TAQ box?" she asked Rodney.

"With Addison. Kimball won't let him or it out of his sight."

"Can you fly a helicopter?"

"No. Can you?"

"No, but I can ride a horse." She nodded at the herdsmen approaching rapidly in a billow of dust and bleating sheep. "Do you suppose we could swap a couple of camels for horses?"

"Maybe. We'd have to be real careful. Nobody trusts anybody around here." Rodney glanced at the flock and frowned again. "Wait a minute. Since when does it take twenty Bedouins to water forty sheep?"

He called something to the guard, just as the lead rider pulled a carbine from a saddle holster and fired into the air. Two more shots rang out and the sheep bolted for the oasis. Over their panicked bleating she heard another handful of shots and the eerie, half-yodeling cries of the herdsmen drawing rifles and heeling their horses into a gallop.

The Arab workmen were shouting, but they weren't firing back. Over her shoulder, Rockie saw them running toward the camels. The Kimball Oil guys rushed out of Mission Control, glanced frantically at the stampeding sheep and charging herdsmen. Two of them pulled pistols, another reached inside for an Uzi.

"Why are they running?" Rockie yelled in Rodney's ear as he grabbed her and pulled her out of the path of the stampede.

"They're locals," he shouted. "They won't shoot their own clansmen and they won't shoot anybody else's unless it's a matter of honor. It'll start a blood feud."

A terrified ewe leapt in front of them, another swerved behind, near enough that Rockie felt the brush of her wool. She flinched at the *ratta-ratta* of the Uzi and the scream of a horse. Gunshots were popping like firecrackers, ringing in her ears and making her heart pound in her throat.

"Where are we going?" she shouted.

"You're going up there." Rodney pointed as they ran, toward the ruins atop the broken outcrop.

"Not without you, I'm not."

"Don't argue, Rockie." Rodney pulled her to a halt on the fringe of the oasis and caught her elbows. "White slavers still operate in this desert. Go before they see you. I'll come for you when it's safe."

He gave her a shove and Rockie went, flying across the rough, rock-strewn depression toward the outcrop. It looked impossibly high, impossible to climb. Conan had said she'd be glad she had her combat boots. Behind her, she could still hear the terrified bleating of the sheep and the blood-curdling cries of the herdsmen over nonstop gunfire. Be careful what you wish for, she reminded herself. She'd wanted out of here, but not this way.

She'd put nearly a hundred yards between herself and the oasis when the fuel dump blew. The shock wave buckled her knees and sent her falling forward. Certain that if she fell she'd never get up again, Rockie stumbled to regain her balance. She heard a scream that sounded like Rodney and spun around at the base of the outcrop.

At the edge of the oasis, a black-robed herdsman reined his mount, a bloodred bay with a dark mane and tail. In the glow of the orange flames leaping behind him, Rockie could see his cuffed leather boots and the dusty mask drawn across his face, gold tassels on the horse's bridle and the gleaming lick of fire on the barrel of the carbine braced on one knee.

Next to Conan, he was the scariest thing she'd ever seen. He turned his head and saw her, shoved his rifle in his saddle holster and kicked the bay into a gallop. Rockie whirled and ran, up the outcrop where she figured the sharp incline would slow the horse up.

It didn't. She glanced over her shoulder and saw the bay leap up the slope after her, its muscled hindquarters bunching with effort. The rider was shouting at her, but she couldn't hear him over the ringing in her ears. Rockie knew it was pointless to keep running, but

Wexlers never quit. She kept zigging and zagging up the rocky, shingled slope until the bay's hoofbeats were thunder in her ears and a strong arm scooped her, kicking and screaming, off her feet.

She rammed her elbows into ribs, drummed her heels against the horse's flanks. The man grunted, the bay whinnied, laid back its ears and wheeled on its hind quarters, half bucking and sliding back down the slope. Rockie pummeled the steely arm encircling her, bowed her back and gave her captor a nasty head butt right in the jaw.

"Ow!" he howled. "Damn it, Rockie, quit it, will you? It's me!"

She froze, hands clenched on his wrist, teeth bared to bite. He sounded like Sheridan, but his voice was muffled by the mask, and she was still mostly deaf. His voice had fooled her before, and she'd already seen one mirage today. What if this was another one? But what if it wasn't?

Holding her breath, Rockie whipped her head around. The face above the dusty black mask was streaked with dirt and soot. The eyes looked brown, but weren't. They were jasper.

"Sherry!" she cried, wrenching the hell out of her back as she twisted and flung her arms around his neck. She buried her face in his shoulder, shaking and shivering with relief. "You aren't a mirage, are you?"

"No," he said gently in her ear. "I'm real."

He smelled like sand and sweat, but Rockie imagined she did, too. She could feel her heart pounding, or maybe it was his. She knew he'd come for the TAQ box, not for her, but it didn't matter. It only mattered that he was here.

The gunfire had all but stopped. An occasional shot rang above the roar of the burning fuel dump, the panicked bleating of the sheep and shrill shouts in Arabic.

"C'mon, Rock," Sheridan said, trying to loosen her arms. "We gotta get outta here."

Rockie peeled herself off his chest, pulled his mask down and touched his cheek. She felt whiskers scrape against her trembling fingers and gave him a quavery smile. "My hero. Leslie of Arabia."

"Egypt," he corrected her with a grin, doubling the reins around his left hand as the bay began to dance. "Maybe Libya for all I know. We're awful close to the border. Hold on while I swing you around."

Rockie did, locking her arm around his neck and kissing him soundly on the mouth. This might be her only chance and she wasn't going to blow it. She wasn't going to spend the rest of her life wondering what his mouth felt like, or if things might've been different if only she'd kissed him when she'd had the chance.

His lips were slack against hers, but only for a heartbeat, only for the second it took him to crush her against him and slant his mouth over hers. He kissed her back, his mouth hard and eager, until the bay snorted and tried to dance out from under them.

Sheridan raised his head, wrapping the reins around his left hand to quiet the horse, looked down at her and smiled. A crooked, one-sided smile, his eyes mostly green.

"I wish you'd done that two days ago," he said, his voice deep and breathless.

"So do I," Rockie murmured, touching his chin with her fingertips.

Another shot rang, close enough to explode a handful of shards from a nearby boulder and startle the bay up on his hindquarters with a frightened whinny. Sheridan whipped his head around, giving Rockie a view over his shoulder of two Kimball Oil guys running toward them from the edge of the oasis.

"Hang on," he said, changing hands with the reins as he lifted and turned her in front of him in the saddle and gave the horse a kick.

With a snort, the bay wheeled away from the oasis at a gallop. Rockie clutched Sheridan's wrist as his left arm slid around her waist, so tightly she could feel his pulsebeat. It was racing, but so was hers.

In the western sky, she saw the first bloody streaks of sunset. This time she'd gotten exactly what she'd wished for. And not a moment too soon.

20

IT WAS DUSK by the time they saw a faint gleam of light, the almost burned-out battery lamp Sheridan had left outside the tiny mud-brick hut hidden at the end of a twisted arroyo in a deep canyon a few miles southeast of the oasis. He'd left the beacon in case he had to find his way back here without Ali, and was damn glad he had.

The exhausted bay gelding raised his head, flared his nostrils and whinnied. A black mare Sheridan could just see running the length of the pole corral like a shadow in the near dark answered.

He should have dismounted long ago. He'd wanted to, but couldn't without letting Rockie see how good she felt sitting on his lap, how thrilling the occasional brush of her breast was against his arm when she shifted against him. The Bedouin clothes Ali had given him to wear were loose, but not loose enough.

The mare stretched her head over the fence and touched muzzles with the gelding as Sheridan drew him to a halt. Rockie sighed and leaned the back of her head against his shoulder. She could feel his breath in her hair and wished he'd touch her. Sheridan wanted to, but didn't.

"I s'pose I have to get down now," she said, "but I'm not sure my legs will work."

"Hold on to me," Sheridan said.

Rockie wrapped her hands around his wrist and swung her right leg over the bay's withers. Sheridan leaned out of the saddle and lowered her to the ground, wincing at the stitch in his bruised ribs.

"Okay?" he asked, holding her against his leg and the bay's hot flanks.

"Yes," Rockie lied, glad it was nearly dark. She didn't want Sheridan to see the tears in her eyes, or how much she wanted to bury her face against his knee and never move.

"There's a privy over there and a jug of water outside to wash with. See it?" Sheridan felt her head turn and nod against his booted calf. "Don't drink it. There's bottled water in the hut. Go inside when you're finished and help yourself. I'll be in as soon as I take care of the horses."

She nodded again and struck off, shivering and rubbing her arms. Already there was a chill in the air. It helped cool Sheridan down. So did waiting until the flimsy wooden door banged shut behind Rockie before swinging his leg over the bay's withers and dropping to the ground. Once he'd tugged the saddle off the tired gelding, he tossed it onto a sawhorse next to the mare's tack and opened the top two corral poles. The bay jumped the bottom one and wheeled away with the mare.

He watered both horses and gave them grain. They plunged into it greedily. They deserved it. The gelding had put in a long day, and both horses had a long night ahead of them.

Sheridan glanced up at the sky as he left the stable, at the first faint stars and the silvery glow of the just-risen moon above the canyon walls. If he and Ali got separated during the raid on the oasis, they'd agreed to meet here when the moon set.

That gave him three, maybe four hours to apologize to Rockie. And make love to her if she'd have him. This might be his only chance, and he didn't intend to blow it. Unless the kiss she'd given him was nothing more than reaction. Or gratitude.

Sheridan stopped off at the privy, then washed off the worst of the sweat and dirt and dried himself with Ali's robe. His teeth were chattering by the time he reached the hut, from anticipation as much as cold.

What if she wouldn't even listen to him? He stopped again, his heart hammering, and remembered that she'd kissed him. It gave him guts enough to push the door open, pick up the burned-out lamp and take it inside.

He wasn't sure what he expected Rockie to do, but turn away from the rickety table and hand him a chipped white coffee cup full of water as he put the lamp down wasn't it. Her hand was trembling. So was his as he took the cup and drained it. She filled it twice more for him from a plastic gallon jug of distilled water.

"Thanks. I needed that."

"Thank you." Rockie put the cap back on the jug but couldn't look at him. "For saving my butt."

"Leslie of Egypt at your service."

Rockie raised just her eyes to his face. His nose and cheekbones were sunburned, his jaw stubbled with whiskers, but he was smiling at her like he had in L.A. If Rockie didn't know better, she'd swear he was glad to see her.

"I'm freezing," she said, because she didn't know what else to say.

"We can't risk a fire, but I've got a camp stove." Sheridan tugged it out from under the table and nodded at the crumbling, lopsided fireplace against one wall. "Sit over there. The embers might still be warm."

They were but just barely. Rockie tried the rough wood floor first, but it was too cold, even on the blanket partially thrown over a saddle with a broken cinch strap. She sat on the single wobbly chair instead, picked up the blanket and threw it over her shoulders.

"Conan wasn't at the oasis," she told Sheridan. "He took the chopper to Cairo to pick up Dad, Kimball and Hanlon."

"I know." Sheridan placed the stove on the uneven hearth and lit it. "Ali's had their camp bugged for months. He works for Max, too. Spying on some of Kimball's locals who are spying for Libya."

"Was Ali one of the herdsmen?"

"Yep. The rest were his cousins. They'll be back once the moon sets, once it's dark enough to move across the open desert safely."

"How did you know where I was?"

"I read Addison's files." Sheridan went back to the table, took several foil packets out of the backpack, hooked the white cup and a blue one over two fingers and picked up the water in his free hand. "He red flagged three sites, oil leases Kimball holds that are about to expire. This one, because of the oasis, was the most logical place to look."

Had he read all the files, Rockie wondered, her heart beginning to race. She opened her mouth to ask, just as he tossed her a couple of the foil packs.

"Trail mix," she said reverently. "I never thought I'd ever be hungry enough to eat this stuff."

Ravenous was a better word, Sheridan thought, watching her rip into a pack. He tossed her the rest, put down the water and the cups, and gathered a pile of threadbare, hand-tied quilts from a wooden bench. He draped one around Rockie, another over himself, a couple more over the saddle, sat down on top of them on the floor and watched her eat.

He changed the battery in the lamp but didn't turn it on. The flames on the little stove made a nice pool of warmth that lit Rockie's tangled dark curls and made them gleam like a raven's wing. She offered him a bag of apple chips, but he shook his head. He was too keyed-up, too aroused.

"Except for airplane food this is all I've had to eat since the eggs I scrambled at your house," she said.

At least he thought that's what she said. She was kind of hard to understand with her cheeks stuffed like a chipmunk, but she kept talking while she ate. She told him how Conan had grabbed her, how they'd gotten here, about the infrared photos and what Rodney Webster had told her about the directional locators and the hut full of explosives she'd seen.

"I figure they're going to use them to generate a seismic wave," she finished. "The way Dad explained it to me I don't think the TAQ box can."

"You figure right," Sheridan replied, filling both cups with water. "Which explains Conan, since explosives are his specialty."

Rockie was afraid of that, but didn't say so. Instead she asked, "Where's Max?"

"Checking out the other two sites with Perry. They should be along around midnight or so."

"I'm glad Perry's okay." Rockie took the blue cup Sheridan handed her and drank.

"So Webster's the one," he said, sipping from the white cup. "Addison knew Kimball had found somebody to check his work. Talk about a viper in your bosom."

The mouthful of water Rockie had just swallowed stuck halfway down. He'd read the letter.

"I suppose," she said slowly, "you could say the same thing about my father."

His arm froze putting the cup down. For just a second, hardly more than an instant, then he completed the motion and leaned his elbow on his raised knee.

"I suppose," he said, staring at the blanket.

"You read the letter."

"Yeah. I read it," Sheridan said curtly. She'd read it, too. He could tell by the quaver in her voice.

"You took a helluva a risk for nothing," she said, ducking her head and picking at a raveled edge of the quilt.

"What d'you mean for nothing?"

"I mean raiding the oasis and coming away without the TAQ box. Rodney told me Kimball won't let it or my father out of his sight."

"I didn't come for the TAQ box."

"You didn't?" Rockie jerked her chin up and blinked at him, surprised. "Then why did you come?"

Sheridan raised his head, his jasper eyes almost green against the mostly blue quilt thrown over him. With a two-day beard and dusty, sweat-spiked hair he was still snatch-your-breath handsome—and that's exactly what he did when he sprang up on his knees, pushed himself between hers and kissed her.

Harder than he meant to, but not nearly long enough. He let her mouth go, wrapped his hands around the back of the chair and looked at her, his heart racing. She blinked back at him, her bottom lip caught between her teeth.

"That's why," he said. "Wanna hit me again?"

"No." She touched his cheek, the scrape of her fingertips on his whiskers shooting a chill up his back. "I want you to kiss me again."

He did, hot and hungry, spreading her knees wider, draping her legs over his hips and gripping the chair again. He kissed her until her lips throbbed, then bent his head and nuzzled her collarbone.

"I'm sorry, Rockie." Sheridan kissed the apology into the hollow of her throat, the pulse he felt beating there sending his own racing. "I'm sorry I didn't do this the first time I wanted to."

"When was that?" She murmured in his ear, her fingers stroking his cheek and shooting shivers through him.

"The first time I saw you."

She laughed, threw her head back and pressed against him. Sheridan groaned, nuzzled her shirt out of his way and grazed his mouth lower. She made a noise in her throat, undid the buttons with shaking fingers and caught her breath as his mouth found her lace-cupped breast.

He circled her nipple with his tongue, heard her whimper and felt her knees clamp around him. He didn't dare do anything else, not yet, but raise his head and look at her.

Her eyes were a soft, misty green in the glow of the stove. He could just see her dusky nipples veiled by white lace and the strawberry flush on the swells of her breasts. He'd put it there, with his whiskers and want. He felt himself throb.

Rockie curved her hand around his cheek, shivering as he turned his head and kissed her palm. "I can't believe we're doing this," she said shakily. "I can't believe I want to. I mean, I can— I mean, I do—"

"There's nothing we can do until the moon sets." Sheridan cut her off with a soft, slow kiss. "Nothing but make up for lost time."

He worked his jaw against her palm, watched her lashes flutter at the scrape of his beard, felt her back arch. He bent his head and gently nuzzled between her breasts, cupped them in his hands as she reached between them and unsnapped her bra.

She spilled into his hands, hot and quivering. Small as she was, her breasts were full. He ran his thumbs around her nipples, felt her melt in his hands, kissed one, then the other, and caught her before she slid off the chair. He picked her up and laid her on the quilts thrown over the saddle, left her shirt on for warmth, stretched her arms over her head and laced his fingers through hers as he eased down on top of her and took her mouth in his.

He felt her shivering but knew she wasn't cold. Her skin was as hot as his. When he kissed her ear, she nipped at his and tugged at his shirt. He went up on his knees and pulled it off. Gooseflesh shot through him, not from cold but the moue she made as she touched the bruises on his chest.

Sheridan caught her hands and pressed them to his heart. She felt it pounding against her palm, caught his left hand and pressed it between her breasts, let him feel her heart thundering along with his. He came to her again and kissed her, nuzzled her ear and said her name, "Rochelle," so softly and with so many *Rs* in it she lost count.

She lost her breath, too, when he rolled his hips against her and murmured something she couldn't understand. He said it again, but she still didn't get it.

"I can't hear you. I'm still deaf from the explosion."

"You're not deaf," Sheridan said with a chuckle. "It's French."

"What's it mean?"

"It means," he said, leaning up on one elbow to look at her, "that I'd like you to take my pants off, then I'd like to take yours off and—"

"Don't tell me." Rockie pressed her fingertips to his lips and smiled. "Show me."

He took off their boots first, threw two quilts over them and braced himself above her on his hands while she untied the drawstring on Ali's billowing trousers. She eased them off with one hand and stroked him with the other, his chest, the small of his back. His arms were shuddering by the time her fingers brushed his hipbones.

It was all he could stand. He rolled on his back and took her with him, sliding her out of her trousers and her panties, nudging himself almost but not quite inside her. She was wet and hot, moaning and shuddering as she cupped his face in her hands and opened her mouth over his.

She kissed him until he couldn't breathe, until what little air he could suck into his lungs rasped in his throat. Then she slithered off him, pulled him over her and opened to take him. He let her, couldn't have stopped her if he wanted to, felt her enclose him and buried himself in velvet fire.

He wanted to go slow, but she wouldn't let him. She writhed beneath him, tightened around him, enflamed him and arched against him when he thrust deeper. Again and again, deeper and harder, locking her legs around him, murmuring his name until she gasped it, clutched him, and he felt her spasm around him. A heartbeat later he shuddered with her, wrapped his arms around her and laid his cheek against the top of her head, spent, shattered and whole again.

It was the best moment of his life, the absolute best. He closed his eyes and savored it, savored her, felt her arms trembling around his neck and wondered what she'd say if he told her he loved her. He wanted to, opened his mouth to tell her, then remembered what awaited them when the moon set. Instead, he said, "You speak French beautifully."

She laughed. He kissed her forehead, leaned up on his elbows and smiled at her. She smiled back and touched his chin with her fingertips.

"I'm not cold anymore."

"You will be if you don't get dressed." Sheridan pulled away from her and reached for a smaller backpack. "I brought you some warm clothes."

He untangled a quilt from his legs and tossed it over her head like a tent. She pushed it out of her eyes and blinked at him like an owl. "I'm not shy. Really."

"I know." He gave her a lingering kiss and flipped the quilt over her face. "Now stay under there until you're dressed and conserve your body heat."

"I'd rather share it," she said, her voice muffled.

"Rockie," he growled, reaching for the jeans and briefs he'd shed before donning his Leslie of Egypt garb.

"All right already."

He heard the backpack zip open and grinned. He pulled on a yellow T-shirt, then a brown-and-gold plaid flannel shirt, and buttoned it. Last, his jeans, socks and boots.

"Where are we going," she asked, "that I have to dress in layers?"

"After Addison and the TAQ box. Conan ought to be back with them from Cairo by now."

And hopping goddamn mad when he discovered the blown fuel dump and realized they were stuck on the oasis. It was part of the plan he and Ali had hatched to trap them with the TAQ box until Max arrived with reinforcements, but he wasn't going to tell Rockie.

She jerked the blanket off her head, gray T-shirt on, black-and-gray flannel shirt unbuttoned. "We're not going back to the oasis, are we?"

"No. I think Kimball plans to blow all three wells. There's a rig on this one you haven't seen yet beyond the escarpment. It's roughly halfway between the other two wells. I figure they'll have to go way, *way* underground to blow them."

"How'er they going to get there?"

"There are miles of tunnels below the ruins."

They were tombs and catacombs, actually, but he wasn't going to tell Rockie. She didn't need to know, since she was never going to see them. Three of Ali's cousins were going to see to it that she stayed here.

"How are we going to get to the ruins without being seen?"

"There's a back way up the outcrop. I brought you something else."

Sheridan smiled, reached into his backpack and pulled out a pack of cigarettes. Her brand.

"Oh, Sherry!" She jumped up on her knees and hugged him, then sat back on her heels and eyed him warily. "You aren't going to make me go outside, are you?"

"No. You can smoke in the house."

She ripped the pack open, shook out a cigarette and grabbed the matches he'd left on the hearth. She didn't realize he'd leaned a Marlboro into the stove and lit it until she struck a match and he blew smoke in her face. Then her mouth dropped open and her cigarette fell onto the blanket. Sheridan picked it up, blew out the match and kissed her.

"I quit three months ago," he said. "Then I met you."

Rockie laughed and hugged him again. Sheridan picked up her cigarette, gave it to her and lit it. She fell back on the saddle, flung out her arms and puffed, then plucked the cigarette from her lips and looked at him.

"Smoking is a filthy, unhealthy habit."

"Absolutely," he agreed, blowing smoke through his nose.

Rockie sat up, folded her legs beneath her and smiled. "I love it," she said softly.

"Me, too," Sheridan murmured and kissed her. "Time to saddle up. Ali will be here soon."

He pulled Rockie up and gave her a sleeveless black corduroy vest. Sheridan shrugged into a quilted brown nylon one and pulled the Cubs hat Rockie had given him out of his backpack. He put it on, swung the rucksack he'd packed with equipment over his shoulder, opened the door and stepped outside.

Sheridan caught only a glimpse of Conan, standing in a pool of moonlight, a smile on his face, an Uzi in his hand, then somebody hit him with something hard and heavy from behind. He went down on his knees, Rockie's scream ringing like an echo in his ears. He knew enough to roll on his back, not to fight to get up.

Gino knew enough to hit him again.

21

HE CAME TO FACEDOWN on cold damp stone, blinked and saw rough-hewn stone walls painted with vivid panels of hieroglyphs. He turned his head carefully and saw Rockie lying on her back on a sleeping bag beside him. Her eyes were closed, her lips parted and her face deathly pale in the flicker of smoking torches in bronze sconces.

He sprang up without thinking and gasped. Pain exploded in his head, but he leaned over Rockie and pressed shaky fingertips beneath her jaw. Her pulse was slow but steady. He sighed with relief and kissed her forehead.

"They drugged her," Addison Wexler said behind him. "You, too, on the way down."

The chamber spun sickeningly as Sheridan whipped his head around. Elbows on his knees, Wexler sat on a slab of pale shaped stone. His tan shirt and trousers were wrinkled, he hadn't shaved recently, his mustache needed trimming, and he had one hell of a black eye.

"And you?" Sheridan asked.

Wexler raised a hand and pointed at his eye. "How d'you think I got this?"

"Lemme guess. So we can't find our way out?"

"Exactly."

"When did you get to be expendable?"

"When my turncoat assistant Rodney Webster told Kimball he'd ironed out the glitch in the directional locators. I installed Rodney's new program before the North Sea test. Dammit to hell." Wexler ran his hand through his mussed-up salt-and-pepper hair. "He botched it worse than I did."

"I take it you told Kimball and he didn't believe you."

"Hell, no. He only believes what he wants to hear."

"Well, well." Sheridan took his crumpled cigarettes out of his pocket and got carefully to his feet to light one in the closest torch. Pain flared in his head again but he ignored it. "At last you know what it's like to work for you."

"They do say what goes around comes around."

Wexler's voice sounded tired and old. Sheridan stood nose to nose with an Egyptian-style figure painted blue with a flesh-and-blood body and a skeleton head. He shivered and turned to look at Wexler. He was staring at Rockie, his chin quavering. The flash of anger Sheridan had felt at his comment faded to a pang of pity.

"Where is everybody?"

"Three, maybe four chambers in that direction." Wexler nodded at a narrow, shadowed archway cut into the wall. "Setting up the TAQ box for the big one."

"How tricky are the passageways?"

"A maze that would astound the architects of Gaza. Four archaeologists that I know of have vanished in here. Who knows how Kimball found the way through, but he did."

Wexler stood up and spread his arms, palms up. His shadow flickered behind him in the torchlight like the wraith of a pharaoh.

"This is the reason Kimball wants the TAQ box. The Egyptian Office of Antiquities has been trying to revoke his lease since they discovered this place. He's managed to tie them up in court so far, but he lost his final appeal three weeks ago. If it's wiped out in a tragic earthquake, he figures they'll renew his lease."

"What a guy." Sheridan shook his head, dragged on his cigarette and glanced up at the ceiling. "Wish I'd dropped bread crumbs on the way down. Any idea how we get out?"

"Teleportation comes to mind," Wexler replied with a thin smile. "Right behind divine intervention."

Rockie moaned. Sheridan glanced at her, saw her frown and roll her head on the sleeping bag.

"Good, she's coming around," he said. "We won't have to carry her out."

"Were you listening to me, Sherry?" Wexler asked incredulously.

"Yeah, I was listening." Sheridan knelt beside Rockie, and closed her right hand in his to raise her body temperature and wake her up.

"We don't have a guard because we don't need one. We haven't a prayer of finding the way out."

Rockie drew a shuddery breath that fluttered her eyelashes. Sheridan kissed her hand, rose and glared at her father.

"What happened to 'Wexlers never quit,' Addison?"

"Why do you keep kissing my daughter?" Wexler demanded, an angry flush creeping up his throat.

"I love her, that's why. I plan to spend the rest of my life loving her, so I'm going to find the way out, and when I do I'm taking you and Rockie with me. I'd just as soon leave you, but she'd kill me and I don't want to die. I'm going to marry her and take her back to Missouri—"

"The hell you are," Rockie croaked groggily. "I'd rather *die* than live in Missouri."

"What a happy coincidence, Rockie," Greer Hanlon said. "You're going to get your wish."

The sound of his voice and footsteps echoing across the chamber cleared the last of the drug from Rockie's brain. She shot to her feet, woozy and off-balance. If her father hadn't caught her, she would have fallen on her face.

"Dad," she breathed, gripping his wrists. The tears in his eyes made her throat ache. She threw her arms around him and gritted her teeth to keep from crying.

"How touching," Hanlon said. "Knock it off and turn around, Rockie."

It was the last thing she wanted to do, but she did it, stepping away from her father and catching Sheridan's hand. She saw Gino and his Uzi first, Hanlon second, and was glad she had something to hang on to. He had no eyebrows or eyelashes. The skin on his forehead was pink and puckered and his toupé had slipped.

"I'm sorry," she said.

"Not yet, but you will be. Come with me."

"Like we've got a choice," Sheridan muttered, lacing his fingers tightly through hers.

Hanlon switched on a flashlight and led them, single file with Gino bringing up the rear, through a series of narrow, unlit passageways that opened into a room so vast Rockie couldn't see the far walls. The roof was low, supported by row after row of columns covered with hieroglyphs. A few held sconces and lit torches.

There was a circle cut in the center of the chamber with eight sets of steps leading down to a massive pillar carved rather than painted with hieroglyphs like the others. Conan stood beside it in a red Kimball Oil jumpsuit, holding two pairs of handcuffs. Next to him sat the TAQ box in its coffin-shaped case, connected by a cable to a notebook computer balanced on Rodney's knees, and wired to a bomb three times as big as the one she and Sheridan had found in the lab.

Rodney sat on one set of steps, typing like a whirlwind with two fingers. He was frowning with concentration and didn't look up until he heard their footsteps.

"This way, Dr. Sheridan, Dr. Wexler," Conan said.

Helplessly, Rockie watched, her heart pounding in her throat, as Gino nudged Sheridan and her father up to the pillar and Conan handcuffed them together around it. She looked at Rodney imploringly. He flushed and dropped his gaze guiltily.

Rockie crammed her hands in the pockets of her corduroy vest to keep them from shaking and felt a sharp prick in her right index finger. She pulled out a dry cleaning tag on a thin wire clip and hastily shoved it back in her pocket. She had no idea how to pick a lock, but she was sure as hell going to try. Just as soon as she figured out how to get close enough to the pillar.

"Where's the boss man?" Sheridan asked, testing the cuffs biting into his wrists.

"On his way back to Cairo," Hanlon said, turning to face them.

"Lisbon might be better," Sheridan replied thoughtfully. "No. Make that Madrid. Yeah, definitely. That's the place to be when this place blows up."

"Oh, please, Sheridan," Hanlon said tiredly. "Wexler's been feeding us that crap for the last week. It's all scientific bullshit."

"We'll find out, won't we?"

"You won't. Neither will Dr. Wexler. Rockie might." He turned his head and smiled at her. "Depends on how nice she is to me."

She jumped, startled, the clip pricking her finger again. Rodney glanced up quickly from his keyboard.

"Funny thing, Rockie," Hanlon went on. "You know, my wife won't even look at me since you did this to my face. I think you owe me."

Oh, God. That's what she'd thought he'd meant. Rockie heard her father moan, watched him thud his forehead against the pillar. Rodney gave up typing and frowned.

"Over my dead body, Hanlon," Sheridan growled.

"Well, naturally. What d'you think, Rockie?"

"I think your wife's a smart woman," she retorted, working the clip straight inside her pocket.

"I think you're a little bitch. I'm going to make you pay like a little bitch, a little bitch in heat, for what you did to me."

"No you're not, Hanlon." Conan took a step away from the pillar. "We have a contract, which clearly states—"

"Your contract is with Kimball," Hanlon cut him off.

"We both work for him, Hanlon. We are both bound by it." There was an edge in Conan's voice, the first time Rockie had ever heard one. "You should have read it. It says that I do not condone nor will I permit rape in my presence."

"Sue me for breach," Hanlon sneered. "Go get her, Gino."

He took two steps before Rodney jumped up from the steps and bashed him over the head with the computer. Rockie didn't wait to watch Gino fall, just bolted for the pillar. Hanlon leapt to intercept her, but Conan cut him off.

From the corner of her eye, Rockie saw him sweep one arm around Hanlon's neck and catch his chin in his other hand, but that's all she saw as she threw herself at Sheridan, clutched his right wrist in her left hand and dug the clip out of her pocket. She'd just managed to insert the tip into the lock when the floor began to shake. So violently she lost the hook and had to grab Sheridan's arm to keep her feet.

"Oh, hell," he said, clutching Rockie's sleeve in his fingers as the pillar groaned and began to shiver.

"Those fools!" Addison Wexler cried. "I told them not to blast. I *told* them!"

"Kimball cancelled the blast order!" Rodney shouted over the screech of tons of stones grinding together, and fell on his knees beside Gino's spread-eagled form. "I heard him."

The floor stopped rolling, but the walls kept groaning. The sound echoed hollowly away through the surrounding chambers. Coughing in the dust sifting out of the ceiling, Rockie dropped to her heels and felt for the wire hook.

"Allow me, Miss Wexler." Conan stepped up beside her, a key ring and a tiny silver key in his big right hand.

Rockie stood up and saw Hanlon sprawled on the floor, his head turned at an unnatural angle. She knew he was dead, knew his neck was broken. She swallowed hard and looked away, stepping clear while Conan unlocked the cuffs.

"Is this a bonafide earthquake, gentlemen?" he asked.

"You damn bet it is," Sheridan snapped, rubbing his wrists. "Ironic as hell, don't you think?"

"I think," Conan replied calmly, "that I should defuse the bomb while you disable the TAQ box, Dr. Sheridan, in case another tremor hits."

"What about your contract with Kimball?"

"Null and void." Conan plucked two screwdrivers from the breast pocket of his jumpsuit and handed one to Sheridan. "Rodney, you start for the surface with Miss Wexler and her father. We'll be along presently."

"No!" Rockie cried, flinging her arms around Sheridan.

"*Yes,*" he said firmly, peeling her off his chest. "Don't be stupid, Rockie. I'll be right behind you."

"Remember what happened the last time you said that to me." Rockie pulled his head down and kissed him fiercely on the mouth. "This time you'd better be right."

"God, you're a pain in the ass." He kissed her back, quickly, then gave her a shove. "Now get outta here."

Rockie went, taking her father's hand and running with him toward the passageway with Rodney, who took a flashlight out of his lab coat pocket and turned it on. Over her shoulder, she watched Sheridan and Conan drop to their knees, one on each side of the TAQ box.

Beyond the beam of the flashlight, the passage was black as the mouth of hell. Which is exactly what this place would be if another tremor struck. Rockie tried not to think about that, just clung to her father's hand.

It seemed to take forever before the maze Rodney led them through started to slant upward. The angle increased with every step, until Rockie's legs began to shudder and she could hear her father's breath rasping behind her.

So suddenly she almost fell on her face, the passageway flattened out and she saw daylight streaming overhead above a crumbling staircase. They stopped a moment to catch their breath, then ran the last twenty yards to the steps and climbed up to the ruined temple on the top of the outcrop.

The view of the desert was stunning. So was the heat and the sight of Egyptian soldiers herding Kimball Oil employees at gunpoint into canvas-topped troop trucks. On the sand at the edge of the oasis sat the Raptor.

"I wonder who tipped them," Rodney said nervously.

"Nevin Maxwell," Rockie said with a sigh of relief, "of Maxwell and Associates, Private Consultations."

"Well, I'll be damned. He came," her father said, then rounded on Rodney. "If you'll do the same, I'll keep quiet about your involvement in this. I'll say you're my assistant, that you were kidnapped with me."

"Thank you, Dr. Wexler," Rodney replied humbly. "It's more than I deserve."

"It's more than both of you deserve," Rockie retorted furiously. "You lied and cheated and connived—"

Her voice cracked and she bit her lower lip. But what did it matter? Would seeing them go to jail make things right? Would it change what happened?

"All right. I'll keep my mouth shut, too, but *only*—" Rockie raised a warning finger "—if Sherry and Maxwell do."

"Fair enough." Addison Wexler gave his daughter a tremulous smile. "That's definitely more than I deserve for what I put you through."

"I'm very, *very* pissed off at you Dad." Rockie shook her finger at him. "But it can wait."

She threw her arms around his neck to hug him, but ended up clinging to him for dear life as the outcrop began to shake beneath them. Dust belched out of the stairwell, a wind-eroded column on the edge of the temple snapped and rolled down the hill.

"Sherry!" Rockie broke away from her father and bolted for the stairs.

"No, Rockie." Rodney caught her and pulled her away. "You can't go back down there."

"The hell I can't! Let me go! Let me—"

A god-awful, bring-up-your-lungs cough and heavy, struggling footsteps cut her off. Rockie wrenched away from Rodney and ran, falling on her knees at the edge of the steps.

"Hello, Miss Wexler." Conan paused halfway up the stairs and smiled at her. His face was filthy, his breathing labored under Sheridan's dead weight thrown across his shoulders.

"Oh, God," Rockie moaned. "Oh, no—"

"Dr. Sheridan will be fine, Miss Wexler." He started up the steps again. "He does, however, need a doctor."

"What happened?" Rockie scrambled out of the way.

"A piece of falling debris struck him." Conan made the last step, went down on one knee and eased Sheridan onto the ground. "I believe he already had a concussion from the blows Gino gave him."

There was blood matted in Sheridan's hair and his face was chalky. Rockie dropped on her knees beside him and kissed his slack mouth.

"We'll get Maxwell," her father said. "C'mon, Rodney."

"Right behind you, sir."

On Sheridan's other side, Conan bent on one knee and raised his limp wrist. He took Sheridan's pulse, his lips moving slightly as he counted seconds through the shattered crystal of his Rolex, laid Sheridan's arm over his chest and lifted his eyelids.

"His pulse is a bit slow, Miss Wexler, but it's strong and steady. His pupils are dilated, however. I urge you to get him to a hospital quickly."

Conan smiled at her and got to his feet. Rockie did, too.

"Thank you," she said, offering him her hand. "Thank you for bringing him back to me."

"You're welcome, Miss Wexler. I have something for you." Conan dropped the cartouche earrings in her palm. "I'd like you to keep them."

"I—" Rockie's voice cracked and her eyes filled as she blinked at the earrings. "I will. Thanks."

He nodded and turned away. On the top of the escarpment behind the ruins, she saw a helicopter crouched like a wasp, a cluster of armed, uniformed men beside it, and remembered Sheridan saying they were awfully close to the border.

"Lemme guess," Rockie said. "Friends of yours from Libya?"

Conan glanced back at her. "It always pays to hedge your bets."

"Wait a minute." She hurried after him. "How did you get out of my father's lab alive?"

"Trade secret, Miss Wexler." Conan paused again and smiled over his shoulder. "Have a happy life."

With any luck, Rockie thought, if she hadn't imagined what Sheridan said about marrying her, she would. "You, too," she told Conan, and meant it.

"You're very young, Miss Wexler." His perpetual smile softened. "And still very naive."

22

JUST LIKE SHE HAD in Barstow, Rockie pushed through the door into Sheridan's hospital room in Aswân at eleven o'clock the next morning. He turned his head on stiff white pillows, saw her and started to smile. Then he remembered who she was and held out his arms.

Rockie wanted to run to him but didn't. He had a concussion and sixteen stitches under the gauze bandage wound around his head. She had a hole in the pit of her stomach, or felt she did.

It was her own fault for lying awake worrying and wondering if he'd really told her father he wanted to marry her. If she'd heard him wrong Rockie wasn't sure what she'd do. After she killed him.

"None of that," she chided sternly, shaking her finger as she walked toward the bed. "You have a concussion."

"A cracked head never killed anybody. Especially me." Sheridan caught her wrist when she came close enough and pulled her onto the mattress beside him. "I've had one for years. It's just official now."

"So's this." Rockie reached for the TV controls and turned the set on to CNN. "He's saying," she explained, as the anchorman spoke in Arabic, "that Winston Kimball, wealthy American oilman, was arrested yesterday in Cairo for attempting to destroy priceless antiquities."

"When did you learn Arabic?"

"Max translated. I've seen this at least thirty times this morning. I memorized it. I'm a quick study."

Rockie smiled proudly. Sheridan frowned.

"What about Addison?"

"Max got him a deal. One for Rodney, too. They're going to be star witnesses for the Department of Antiquities. They'd love to go home, but they're going to be here a while."

Sheridan's frown deepened. Rockie felt her smile slip. The vivid Egyptian sun slanting through the window beside the bed picked up the reddish flecks in his eyes. Not a good sign.

"What about you?" Sheridan asked, dread knotting his stomach. "Are you going to stay here with Addison?"

"Are you kidding?" Rockie pressed her left hand to the base of her throat. "It's hot and dangerous and I don't speak Arabic. Egypt has only one thing going for it that I can see."

"What's that?"

"It's not Missouri."

Sheridan grabbed for her, but she scooted nimbly off the bed and grinned at him. Her hair was spiked again. So was the turquoise leather bracelet she wore on her left wrist. It matched her skirt and her Hell's Angels jacket. Sheridan wondered what his mother would say when he told her his bride-to-be wore combat boots and bought her clothes at Bikers R Us.

"I brought you something." Rockie swung the patchwork tote off her shoulder and pulled out a Cubs hat with the price tag still dangling from the back. "Anybody ever told you you're hard on hats?"

"How in hell," Sheridan said with a laugh, "did you find a Cubs hat in Egypt?"

"Don't ask." Rockie sat down beside him again, bit the tag off and put it on his head, gingerly easing it over the bandage. "You look like a mummy. How much hair did they shave off?"

"We're going to be an interesting couple for a while." Sheridan caught her hand and laced their fingers together. "A biker and a Hare Krishna."

A couple, Rockie thought, her heart beginning to race with excitement. We're going to be a couple. Sheridan smiled at her, the stroke of his thumb across her knuckles making her shiver. She ached to kiss him, to feel his arms around her. If he didn't hurry up and ask her to marry him she was going to have to ask him. Or smother him.

"I like your earrings." Sheridan touched one of the gold cartouches swinging from her ears and felt her fingers tremble. "Should I ask where you got 'em?"

"Not a good idea." Not now, Rockie thought. She'd tell him. Eventually. He needed time to heal and so did she. "I can't decide what to call you. Leslie or Sherry?"

Sheridan smiled. He'd been waiting for an opening, had spent the whole morning practicing clever proposals.

"How about husband?"

At last, Rockie wanted to scream. She wanted to fling herself into his arms, too, but decided to make him sweat.

"Do I have to live in Missouri to call you that?"

Sheridan had been thinking about that, too. He had an answer ready, but he made her wait. He could see her pulse skipping in the hollow of her throat and wanted to kiss it.

"Not necessarily. So long as you're willing to call me husband some place where they don't have earthquakes."

Rockie tossed back her head and laughed. Sheridan had seen her eyes glitter with fear and mist with desire—for him, for now and forever, he hoped to God—but decided he liked this happy, deep emerald sparkle best.

"What's so funny?" he asked her.

"You," Rockie said, wiping tears off her eyelashes. "The big, brave, quake-shy geologist."

"Don't forget looter and pain in the ass," Sheridan reminded her with a grin.

"How could I forget. Which reminds me. I asked Dad about the island and the MPs he mentioned in his letter, but he said I should ask you."

"Good old Addison," Sheridan said sourly. "Would you be real ticked off if we didn't invite him to the wedding?"

"Very ticked off." Rockie leaned over him on her right arm. "C'mon, tell me."

"Promise you'll marry me anyway?"

"You haven't asked me yet."

"Will you marry me?"

"Yes. Now tell me."

"Okay, okay," Sheridan grumbled. "To make a long story short, I sunk it."

Rockie blinked at him, puzzled. "What did you sink?"

"The whole damn island," Maxwell said from the doorway.

Rockie glanced over her shoulder, saw the door swing shut behind him and the grin on his face that almost reached his cobalt eyes. She heard Sheridan groan and felt him slide lower in the bed.

"What island?" she asked.

"It didn't have a name." Maxwell came to the foot of the bed and tucked his hands in the pockets of his pleated beige linen trousers.

He looked more relaxed than Rockie had ever seen him, the sleeves of his ivory silk shirt rolled to the elbow, the top two buttons undone. Something gold and wafer thin hung from a fine gold chain around his neck, but she couldn't see what.

"It was an atoll, really," Maxwell went on, "just a lump of sand in the backwater of the Pacific where the U.S. Navy wisely sent your father and Mr. Wizard to do six months worth of cutting-edge research on quake detection. I was their one man security detail. I woke up one night in what I thought was the throes of an erotic dream, only to find my cot floating in three feet of seawater."

"Oh, no," Rockie said, trying not to grin. "Don't tell me it was the TAQ box."

Maxwell nodded. "The very first prototype."

Sheridan groaned again and slid lower. Rockie glanced at him, saw that he'd pulled his Cubs hat over his eyes, then back at Maxwell. She couldn't believe the almost twinkle in his cobalt eyes, or that she wanted to laugh about something that had caused so much grief and destruction.

"It's okay, Rockie." Maxwell smiled at her. "It *was* funny at the time."

"Until my father got his hands on the TAQ box," she said solemnly.

"C'mon, Rock. Buck up." Sheridan pushed himself up in the bed, his cap off his face and turned her chin toward him. "I think Addison has learned his lesson. God knows I have. No more monkeying with Mother Nature for me."

"There will be a few million questions for you to answer in Cairo when they let you out of here tomorrow," Maxwell said. "I'll fly you up with Rockie. Addison and Rodney are leaving with the Antiquities officials this afternoon. Addison would like to see you before he leaves, Rockie, but he knows you'll want to stay here with Sherry."

"He does?" she asked, feeling herself flush.

"Even I know." Maxwell laid a surprisingly gentle hand on her shoulder. "Send me an invitation to the wedding."

"I will," Rockie promised. "Just as soon as we figure out a place to have it that doesn't have earthquakes."

"I need a best man, Max," Sheridan said, "and you're the best one I know."

"I can't, Sherry. Not even for you." Maxwell gave him a smile that came nowhere near his eyes. "I'll wait for you outside, Rockie. No rush. When you're ready, I'll drive you back to the hotel."

"Don't ask," Sheridan warned, when the door closed behind Maxwell.

"I wasn't going to," Rockie lied, figuring she'd worm it out of him later. "I was going to kiss you."

"At long last." Sheridan sighed and opened his arms.

Rockie slipped into them, parting her lips as he bent his head and slanted his mouth over hers. He slid his fingers into her hair, his tongue under hers, kissed and stroked her until she could scarcely draw a breath.

"I never knew cigarettes could taste so sexy," Sheridan groaned, dragging his mouth from her lips to her ear. "You didn't bring me one, did you?"

Rockie laughed. Sheridan cupped her face in his hands and felt his throat swell as he gazed into her deep green emerald eyes. At last he'd found a Wexler who knew how to give. Better than she got, more than he deserved.

"I'm one lucky pain in the ass," he told her softly.

"Me, too." Rockie nestled her head on his chest and listened contentedly to his heart beat beneath her ear. "You were kidding about my father and the wedding, weren't you?"

"'Course I was," Sheridan lied, stroking her cheek with his curved knuckles.

"I love you, Sherry."

He kissed the top of her head. "I love you, Rockie."

"I love you, Leslie."

"I said I love you, Rockie."

"Don't get cranky. I'm just trying to find one I like." She raised her head, pursed her lips for a moment, then grinned at him, her green eyes shining. "I love you, Bullwinkle."

Join the festivities as Harlequin celebrates Temptation's tenth anniversary in 1994!

Look for tempting treats from your favorite Temptation authors all year long. The celebration begins with Passion's Quest—four exciting sensual stories featuring the most elemental passions....

The temptation continues with Lost Loves, a sizzling miniseries about love lost...love found. And watch for the 500th Temptation in July by bestselling author Rita Clay Estrada, a seductive story in the vein of the much-loved tale, THE IVORY KEY.

In May, look for details of an irresistible offer: three classic Temptation novels by Rita Clay Estrada, Glenda Sanders and Gina Wilkins in a collector's hardcover edition—free with proof of purchase!

After ten tempting years, *nobody* can resist

Temptation®

HT10AN

INDULGE A LITTLE 6947 SWEEPSTAKES
NO PURCHASE NECESSARY

HERE'S HOW THE SWEEPSTAKES WORKS:
The Harlequin Reader Service shipments for January, February and March 1994 will contain, respectively, coupons for entry into three prize drawings: a trip for two to San Francisco, an Alaskan cruise for two and a trip for two to Hawaii. To be eligible for any drawing using an Entry Coupon, simply complete and mail according to directions.

There is no obligation to continue as a Reader Service subscriber to enter and be eligible for any prize drawing. You may also enter any drawing by hand printing your name and address on a 3" x 5" card and the destination of the prize you wish that entry to be considered for (i.e., San Francisco trip, Alaskan cruise or Hawaiian trip). Send your 3" x 5" entries to: Indulge a Little 6947 Sweepstakes, c/o Prize Destination you wish that entry to be considered for, P.O. Box 1315, Buffalo, NY 14269-1315, U.S.A. or Indulge a Little 6947 Sweepstakes, P.O. Box 610, Fort Erie, Ontario L2A 5X3, Canada.

To be eligible for the San Francisco trip, entries must be received by 4/30/94; for the Alaskan cruise, 5/31/94; and the Hawaiian trip, 6/30/94. No responsibility is assumed for lost, late or misdirected mail. Sweepstakes open to residents of the U.S. (except Puerto Rico) and Canada, 18 years of age or older. All applicable laws and regulations apply. Sweepstakes void wherever prohibited.

For a copy of the Official Rules, send a self-addressed, stamped envelope (WA residents need not affix return postage) to: Indulge a Little 6947 Rules, P.O. Box 4631, Blair, NE 68009, U.S.A.

INDR93

INDULGE A LITTLE 6947 SWEEPSTAKES
NO PURCHASE NECESSARY

HERE'S HOW THE SWEEPSTAKES WORKS:
The Harlequin Reader Service shipments for January, February and March 1994 will contain, respectively, coupons for entry into three prize drawings: a trip for two to San Francisco, an Alaskan cruise for two and a trip for two to Hawaii. To be eligible for any drawing using an Entry Coupon, simply complete and mail according to directions.

There is no obligation to continue as a Reader Service subscriber to enter and be eligible for any prize drawing. You may also enter any drawing by hand printing your name and address on a 3" x 5" card and the destination of the prize you wish that entry to be considered for (i.e., San Francisco trip, Alaskan cruise or Hawaiian trip). Send your 3" x 5" entries to: Indulge a Little 6947 Sweepstakes, c/o Prize Destination you wish that entry to be considered for, P.O. Box 1315, Buffalo, NY 14269-1315, U.S.A. or Indulge a Little 6947 Sweepstakes, P.O. Box 610, Fort Erie, Ontario L2A 5X3, Canada.

To be eligible for the San Francisco trip, entries must be received by 4/30/94; for the Alaskan cruise, 5/31/94; and the Hawaiian trip, 6/30/94. No responsibility is assumed for lost, late or misdirected mail. Sweepstakes open to residents of the U.S. (except Puerto Rico) and Canada, 18 years of age or older. All applicable laws and regulations apply. Sweepstakes void wherever prohibited.

For a copy of the Official Rules, send a self-addressed, stamped envelope (WA residents need not affix return postage) to: Indulge a Little 6947 Rules, P.O. Box 4631, Blair, NE 68009, U.S.A.

INDR93

INDULGE A LITTLE
SWEEPSTAKES

OFFICIAL ENTRY COUPON

This entry must be received by: APRIL 30, 1994
This month's winner will be notified by: MAY 15, 1994
Trip must be taken between: JUNE 30, 1994-JUNE 30, 1995

YES, I want to win the San Francisco vacation for two. I understand that the prize includes round-trip airfare, first-class hotel, rental car and pocket money as revealed on the "wallet" scratch-off card.

Name______________________________

Address ____________________ Apt. ____________

City______________________________

State/Prov.____________ Zip/Postal Code____________

Daytime phone number______________________________
(Area Code)

Account #______________________________

Return entries with invoice in envelope provided. Each book in this shipment has two entry coupons—and the more coupons you enter, the better your chances of winning!

 MONTH1

INDULGE A LITTLE
SWEEPSTAKES

OFFICIAL ENTRY COUPON

This entry must be received by: APRIL 30, 1994
This month's winner will be notified by: MAY 15, 1994
Trip must be taken between: JUNE 30, 1994-JUNE 30, 1995

YES, I want to win the San Francisco vacation for two. I understand that the prize includes round-trip airfare, first-class hotel, rental car and pocket money as revealed on the "wallet" scratch-off card.

Name______________________________

Address ____________________ Apt. ____________

City______________________________

State/Prov.____________ Zip/Postal Code____________

Daytime phone number______________________________
(Area Code)

Account #______________________________

Return entries with invoice in envelope provided. Each book in this shipment has two entry coupons—and the more coupons you enter, the better your chances of winning!

© 1993 HARLEQUIN ENTERPRISES LTD. MONTH1